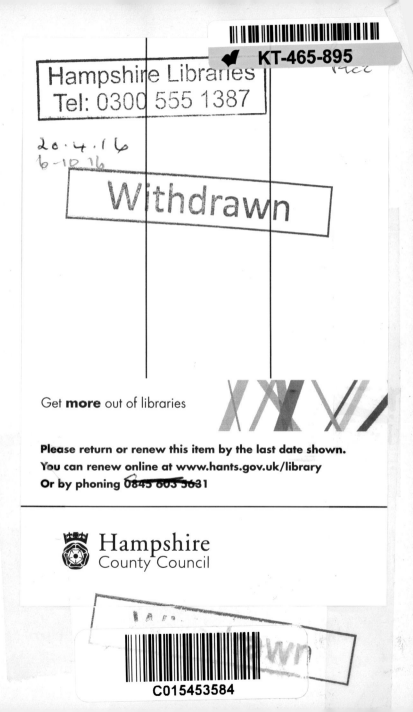

THE SURGEON'S MISTAKE

Matti Harper has been in love with Ian Faulkner since their school days. He is now an eminent cardiac surgeon, she his theatre nurse. Ian has finally fallen in love — the trouble is, it's with Matti's flatmate Lori! But whilst a heartbroken Matti prepares to be their bridesmaid, Lori is being suspiciously flirtatious with another man. How can Matti tell Ian without appearing to be jealous? Best man Sam Grayling tries to help, but only succeeds in sending things from bad to worse . . .

CHRISSIE LOVEDAY

THE SURGEON'S MISTAKE

Complete and Unabridged

LINFORD
Leicester

First published in Great Britain in 2013

First Linford Edition
published 2014

A catalogue record for this book is available
from the British Library.

ISBN 978–1–4448–2226–7

Set by Words & Graphics Ltd.
Anstey, Leicestershire
Printed and bound in Great Britain by
T. J. International Ltd., Padstow, Cornwall

This book is printed on acid-free paper

1

'Think that's about it,' Ian said as he finished operating. 'Another one mended for a few more years, hopefully. Thanks everyone. Good job.' There was a murmur round the room as they acknowledged the surgeon's words. He was the best in the hospital and everyone enjoyed working alongside him.

Matti followed him into the outer room and watched as he stripped off his operating gown and the ridiculous hat. He was the top cardiac surgeon, young enough to be adored by most of the female staff in the hospital. She was the head theatre nurse, who always worked closely with the man, Mr Ian Faulkner. He turned and grinned at her. The dark grey eyes crinkled at the corners in the same way they had when he was in the year above her at school. His smile revealed perfect white teeth. The years had turned the schoolboy into one gorgeous man.

'Dear Matti. You know, I can't believe I'm getting married in just over a week,' he said softly, touching her arm. She looked at the long fingers that were so capable and talented. She shivered. Damn the man. Why did he have this effect on her?

'I can't believe it either.' She turned away, hoping the tears pressing at the back of her eyes didn't explode onto her cheeks. Getting married. Her Ian, the man she had loved since she was a teenager, was about to marry her own friend and flatmate. And she had actually introduced them. More fool her. What was it? Six weeks? Only six weeks ago? And tonight was Lori's hen night. She could hardly believe this was happening. Somehow, she had to get through it. Still, it would be good practice for the actual wedding day, which could only be a million times worse. She felt Ian's hand on her arm and gave another shiver.

'Matti . . . I just wanted to thank you

2

for everything you've done for us and please, take care of Lori tonight. I know she's looking forward to her party but I also know she can go a bit wild.' He put his arms round her and gave her a brotherly hug. Only to her, it was anything but brotherly. She managed to croak back,

'Course I'll look out for her. I'm chief bridesmaid, aren't I? It's my job.'

'Thanks, love.' He planted a kiss on her forehead and bounded out of the theatre. She dumped her own theatre garb into the basket and went along the corridor to the staff room. She flopped down in an easy chair, feeling drained. Why had she never told Ian how she felt? Now it was much too late. What a wimp she was.

* * *

Matti watched as her friend cavorted round the room wearing a silly plastic tiara with a froth of white lace attached. Her gorgeous deep red hair bounced round her shoulders and she had to admit, the bride-to-be looked stunning. No wonder Ian had fallen for her. The other girls were sporting pink feathery wings and beginning to sing in loud, cracked voices. She tried hard to enter the spirit of the occasion but how could she hide a heart that was breaking in two? Lori was about to marry Ian. Her Ian. And there was nothing she could do about it.

'Come on, Matti. You've got by far the best voice of any of us. Get up on that stage, grab the mike and sing to us.'

'Sorry . . . I've got a sore throat,' she claimed.

'Rubbish. We've all got sore throats and undoubtedly our heads will be sore in the morning. Whoops,' Lori cried out as she crashed into a table.

'Steady on. It's my job as chief bridesmaid to keep you fully intact for the big day. You'll have a colossal bruise on your arm. Not a good look with that gorgeous dress you've chosen.'

'Matti, you're too good to me,' Lori slurred as she flung her arm round her friend.

'Too right I am,' Matti whispered. 'Maybe you need to slow down a bit?'

'Nonsense. There's a week to go before the wedding. I shall remain sober for an entire week after tonight. More champagne please.' She grabbed an empty glass from the table and held it out for a refill. Matti grabbed a bottle of sparkling water and poured it into the bride-to-be's glass.

'Thank you, darling. Lovely bubbles. Can't have too much champagne.' She hiccupped loudly and sat down heavily. Mattie refilled Lori's glass with mineral water. Perhaps she was taking her role as chief bridesmaid too seriously. Everyone else was feeling merry with the liberal supplies of alcohol provided by the bride's doting father, and she was herself totally sober. She never drank much but on this occasion, she knew that her early start next day meant she had to be abstemious.

People's lives might depend on it.

'I can always get blitzed at the wedding, once the reception starts,' she decided.

At last the evening was drawing to a close, much to Mattie's relief. One event over, and this time next week she would actually be helping Lori to prepare to marry Ian. She just had to accept it. He had made his choice, even if her own heart was gradually falling into pieces. She held her head high and told herself that she must get through it. Maybe there was someone special waiting round the corner and it was only a matter of time before she would fall in love with a man who really wanted her.

'I love you, Matti.' Lori's voice was slurred and her eyes rolled drunkenly. 'You're a wonderful friend. Best ever. So generous. I know you cared for Ian, way before we met, but it never stopped you being my friend.' Lori was leaning heavily against her in the taxi. Matti was praying she wasn't sick before they reached the flat they shared. 'Maybe you'll fall in love with the gorgeous Sam Grayling. He's going to be the best man, you know, and bridesmaids and best mans always fall in love.' Another hiccup but fortunately, nothing worse.

'This is the place,' Matti told the cab driver. 'Thanks. If you just stop here.' She pulled out her purse and paid the fare, adding a generous tip to make up for the lateness of the hour.

'Hope you manage to sober her up in time for the ceremony,' he laughed. 'Thanks, love, and don't forget your wings. You may need them to catch up with the bride.'

She hauled her friend up the stairs and helped her onto the bed. Removing the shoes and tiara, Matti left Lori to sleep it off. Two o'clock. She had five hours to catch some sleep and then she would be on duty at the hospital. Thank goodness she had a clear head and her only symptoms were weariness. She left Lori to her hangover.

Saturday mornings were no different

from any other day on the cardiac unit. Though they didn't always have scheduled operations for the day, there were often emergencies and other patients to be examined before moving them from intensive care to HDU, the high dependency unit. At eight o'clock she went to change into scrubs in the staff changing room.

'Hi, how did it go?' Matti's heart pounded as Ian came into the room. 'Coffee? Strong and black I presume?'

'Coffee would be great. Just as normal though. I didn't drink a thing last night. More than I can say for your fiancée, however. She was still snoring it off when I left.'

'Well done you. I'll give her a call later. There you go. One coffee, just as you like it.'

Matti forced a smile. 'Thanks. Just what I need. I didn't stop for breakfast this morning.'

'Then I shall get a muffin for you. Can't have you collapsing on us.' He put a hand on her arm and Mattie winced. He shouldn't be doing this to her. Not when he'd decided to marry her friend.

'You all right?' he asked. His dark grey eyes looked anxiously into her own blue ones. His hand brushed away the stray dark lock that frequented his forehead. 'Come on my pretty one, tell Uncle Ian what's wrong.'

She swallowed away the threatening tears. 'I'm fine. Just tired. Now, are you getting that muffin or shall I just quietly starve to death?'

'That's my girl. Always ready with a joke.'

'This is no joke. I need calories and fast. Before we start saving other people's lives, I need my own to be saved.'

He gave her a peck on the cheek and went off to the canteen. She touched the spot and wondered if anything could ever be the same again. They'd known each other since school days. They'd been to the same university but followed different courses. Friendly rivalry had lead to a close friendship. One that she'd always thought . . . hoped . . . would turn into something much more. That was before Lori had arrived at the hospital wearing her neat nurse's uniform and a big smile. Lovely, lively Lori. They had become friends and decided to share a flat together. Once Lori had met Ian, the rest was history, as they say. Evidently Lori had fallen hook line and sinker for the man she believed was a sort of honorary brother to her flat-mate. Matti laughed ironically. She had never dreamed it would go this far between the pair. After a whirlwind few weeks, that was it. A bit of fun and flirting, but never marriage between the two of them. Ian seemed almost as shocked as she was at the speed with which it all happened. He had been singled out. Lori always had heaps of friends, many of them males. In fact, Matti began to wonder what she and Lori actually had in common. She preferred a relatively quiet life while Lori was always out partying. She loved reading and music and going to concerts rather than the noisy club routine favoured by Lori. Ian disliked clubs too, so their sudden marriage plans seemed even more unlikely.

Matti saw Ian coming back and hauled her brain back to the present. His tall frame shadowed over the door. She took a deep breath to calm herself and fixed a smile on her face.

'Saved in the nick of time. Double chocolate chip, I hope.'

His face fell. 'They'd sold out. It's a healthy wheat fibre slice. Much better for you.'

'Okay. It'll have to do. It's truly a double choc chip day, though.' She opened the bag and there was a large double chocolate chip muffin. 'Rotter,' she laughed.

'More than my life's worth to deprive you of a chocolate fix. Right, well, enjoy. See you on the ward in a few minutes.'

He went into the office and looked through his notes. He thought about Matti. She was such a big part of his life. He hoped they would still be friends. Funny, at one time he'd wondered if there might be something more between them, but she had treated him more like a big brother. She was a lovely woman with a direct gaze and clear blue eyes. Her long blonde hair was always neatly coiled for work and rarely did she have a single strand out of place. He had at one time fantasised about pulling out the pins and letting it fall loose down her back. He'd smiled. One of those old movies where the doctor said, 'Why, Miss Harper, you're beautiful' and the heroine fell into the arms of the hero. But that was not real life. He already knew Matti was beautiful both inside and outside. He loved working with her as she had great rapport with the patients and often calmed them where he failed to do so, with his more clinical approach. Life with Matti would certainly be less stressful. He'd fallen for Lori's vitality and she had claimed him for her own very soon after they'd met. It was very flattering and unexpected but she was a beautiful girl.

Why didn't he ever call her a woman? he suddenly wondered. She was truly just a girl. A vibrant sexy girl, with a joy of life that she seemed to spread to those around her. She was sometimes a bit scatty but as far as he knew, she did her work well enough and the patients seemed to enjoy her company, even if she was frequently late for her shifts. Her colleagues always covered for her with good will, for some unknown reason. She was always rushing somewhere, always had someone she must see right away. Something she must do immediately. It could at times be irritating but he felt sure she loved him and he loved her. And they both loved Matti, dear dependable Matti.

He picked up the files and prepared for another busy day. All this was quite out of character for him but he was swept along by the whirlwind that was Lori. Right or wrong, he hadn't stopped long enough to catch breath.

'Thanks for the muffin,' Matti whispered as she caught up with him next to the bed of Mr Jones, the man who had been operated on the previous day. Ian winked at her with a conspiratorial nod. Her heart lifted for a second.

'How are you feeling today?' he asked the patient.

'Bit under the weather. Not quite sure where I am. Feel as if I've been run over by a steam roller.' His voice was shaky but he managed a feeble smile.

'You're doing really well. Confusion is quite common. It's the medication and you have had major surgery after all.' He looked at the computerised dials surrounding the bed. 'But, you'll be pleased to know that everything seems to be working properly. We did a quadruple bypass in the end. Four of your arteries needed replacing. You'll start to feel much better soon. The sister will help you out of bed in a little while.'

'Really, Doc? Didn't think I'd be moving much today.'

'Oh yes. It's important we get you moving soon. Have you eaten yet?'

'They asked if I wanted something but . . . ' He shook his head as if it was all too much effort.

'Well, you try to eat something when you're ready. It all helps you to feel better. You know about the pain killers? How to use the pump?' Mr Jones nodded. He'd been shown how to push the button on the pump for pain relief when he felt discomfort. A dose was released immediately and monitored on the sophisticated equipment. It was impossible to take an overdose as everything was automatically logged. For the first few hours, a dedicated nurse was looking after him alone and also recording on a chart everything that happened. It was all checked and double-checked so there was no room for error.

'Thanks Doc.' He looked at Matti. 'Don't I know you from somewhere?'

'We met yesterday. In the theatre.'

'Lucky me. Taking a pretty girl to the theatre.'

'Try to rest now. We'll see you later,' Mattie said with a smile.

The next patient appeared to be asleep. Ian glanced at the notes. The dedicated nurse appeared at his side.

'Anything wrong here?' Ian asked.

'I'm not sure. Functions are relatively normal for the condition but I suspect there may be something going on we can't see.'

'Okay. Keep me posted. I won't disturb him now. Anything else to report?'

The nurse shook his head. 'I'll bleep you if I need to.'

The rest of the round went as normal and by midday they were able to take a coffee break.

'So, tell me about last night,' Ian prompted. 'Did Lori disgrace herself?'

'Not really. She was rather drunk but eventually I managed to convince her that sparkling mineral water was champagne so we were spared the worst.'

'She does enjoy her drinks doesn't she?' he said quietly. 'I worry about her sometimes.'

'She just enjoys life,' Matti said with a degree of loyalty she did not feel. Lori often went out in an evening and never said where she was going. She stopped herself from saying anything to Ian in case it might sound like jealousy. She sometimes felt that she was living an incredibly boring life and was wasting opportunities. But she was Matti — sensible, tolerant old Matti, who took her work too seriously. Maybe it was time for a change.

'I guess. I'm going to grab an early lunch. Want to join me?' Ian suggested.

'Well, if I won't be in the way. Thanks.'

They went to the canteen together, chatting about patients, work and anything other than the forthcoming wedding. They took their trays to a side table, away from the general hubbub of the busy room.

'Can I join you?' asked the good-looking blond doctor, Sam Grayling, and Ian's best-man-to-be.

'Sure, pull up a seat. How's life in

paediatrics? Oh, you know Matti of course? She's my right-hand man in the theatre. Best theatre sister in the business.'

'Yes, of course. We've met. I believe we have compatible roles in this wedding next week?'

'I think so. Hope you manage this chap better tonight than I did my charge last night.'

'Oh, we intend to have fun tonight, don't we, my boy? You'll have the rest of the weekend to recover.'

'I'm not sure about that. I may have to come back to look at one of my patients. Bit of a problem.'

'No way. You're not on call and believe it or not, there are other fully competent surgeons available.' Sam seemed as nice as she'd heard, Matti decided. He wasn't darkly handsome like Ian and wasn't as tall but he had merry blue eyes and a wicked grin. She'd seen him around of course, but he worked in paediatrics and their paths had rarely crossed professionally.

'So, what happened to the bride last night?' he asked.

'Nothing too outrageous, actually. She went a bit heavy on the champagne and as far as I know, she's still sleeping it off.'

'How about you and I get together one evening during this next week? We need to compare notes ready for next Saturday. How about I take you out to dinner on Monday evening?'

'Well, thanks. If you're sure. I mean you don't have to . . . '

'Course I don't have to, but it's the best excuse I've come up with to ask a gorgeous woman for a date.'

'Just watch him, Matti. He's lethal. The blue eyes may look innocent but they hide a dangerous interior.'

'Watch it, you,' Sam said as he poked his friend. They had such an easy rapport, it was clear the two men were really good friends. So why hadn't Matti ever met him properly before? It might make the wedding easier to bear if she had an ally. 'So what do you say,

Matti? A quiet dinner somewhere on Monday and we can hatch our strategies for this coming shindig?'

'Okay. Thanks. I'd like that.'

'I'll take the opportunity to give you the lowdown on this terrible man,' he offered.

'She doesn't need to be told anything about me. We were at school together and then Uni and we've been working together for the last two years.'

'Good heavens, and you haven't snapped her up in all that time? What's wrong with you, man? Still, I suppose the lovely Lori came along and bagged you for herself. Though what women see in you, I'll never . . . '

'That's quite enough, thank you.' Ian's pager went off. 'Sorry. I've got to go. Think it's the patient I was worried about. Finish your lunch, Matti, and then come straight to the ward. I suspect we shall be going back to theatre.'

'Far too dedicated, that one,' Sam said cheerfully.

'From what I've heard, you're hardly

one to talk,' said Ian. 'I've heard about your all-night stints when a child is causing concern.' With that, he left the canteen.

'Is there nothing secret in this place? These gossip lines are the hottest network going. So, what do you really think about this marriage?' Sam said, turning to Matti. 'I mean, you obviously know both bride and groom pretty well.'

'I suppose they . . . well, they seem to be in love, I guess.'

'All happened much too fast for my taste. One minute Ian's steadily working away, enjoying life, and the next he's evidently been swept off his feet and is getting married. Two or three weeks is all it is and he's planning to spend the rest of his life with the woman?'

Matti bit her lip. Exactly what she thought. 'But if they're really in love, why wait?'

'You say if they are in love. Not that they love each other. And there's a big 'if' in my book.'

'And the difference is?' Her own pager went off. 'Sorry. I'll have to go.'

'Give me your mobile number. I'll call you later about that dinner. I shall look forward to getting to know you.' She rattled off the numbers as she collected her empty plates together to take to the clearing stands.

She rushed back to the ward, her mind churning over Sam's words. He was actually voicing all the doubts she felt inside. She had been constantly putting those doubts down to her own jealousy, but had Ian really fallen for an image? An image that Lori presented? Was he making the worst mistake of his entire life? She needed to talk it over with someone very soon. Sam? He seemed a distinct possibility and very dishy in a different way. Perhaps he might even help her come to terms with her loss of Ian.

2

The cardiac ward was quiet except for the gentle bleeping of many monitors and discreet voices consulting over each of the patients. They usually stayed in the intensive care unit for twenty-four hours and if progress was satisfactory, patients moved to the high dependency unit next door. Everything was very controlled; visitors were only admitted at the ward sister's discretion and only then after a screening process. There were several people standing around the bed of Mr Palmer, however. The ward sister herself and two other nurses were trying to keep the patient calm, while Ian was attempting to persuade him that a further trip to the theatre was essential. A woman, presumably his wife, was hovering at the back of the group, looking terrified. Matti moved close to them. The woman turned and went over to her.

'I don't understand what they're saying. That's my husband there. Something about a drain not working or being blocked. They said he was doing all right this morning when I rang and as soon as I got here, they all seemed to be crowding round him and looking worried. What's going on?'

'I'll see what I can find out. Why don't you take a seat over by the desk there? I'll come and talk to you as soon as I know anything.' She went to the bedside and listened to the conversation.

'I quite understand that you don't want to go through surgery again, Mr Palmer, but we think there's a bleed inside. We don't know exactly where it's coming from and we need to check it out. Sister will give you something to make you feel sleepy and we'll soon sort you out.' Ian spoke in his usual calm and no-nonsense way. People did not argue with him.

'Can you have a word with his wife?

Or shall I do it?' Matti asked.

'Do you mind doing it? I need to get the theatre set up. Have a word with her and then come and join me. I'm hoping it's nothing much but we have to be certain. It's getting on for twenty-four hours since the op so it should be settling by now.'

Calmly, Matti explained to the terrified wife that the problem her husband was experiencing was something that often happened. 'Occasionally the sutures — the stitches — haven't quite held. And it's very much easier to do the checks at this stage before the healing process has really started.'

'But it's already such a great big wound he has.'

'Believe me, you'll be surprised by how quickly it will fade and shrink. Much better to do it now and be certain everything is as it should be. It's much worse if we wait till the healing has really begun properly. Now, do you want to speak to your husband before he goes to theatre?'

'All right then. Thank you. Where shall I wait?'

'The sister will advise you. She may suggest you might like to go home. He will be in theatre for quite some time and then he'll be very sleepy for a long time afterwards. There's nothing you can do and she can phone you with every stage of the process. All right? I'll see you later.'

She turned and left the ward, making for the theatre. It was a fairly new wing and all the necessary facilities were close by and very practical and stream-lined. Everything was prepared in theatre; the anaesthetist was standing by and Ian was already gowned. Matti scrubbed and gowned in a short time and was standing by, ready for the patient's arrival.

'Sorry you have to undo your fine needlework,' she said from behind her mask.

'Hopefully we shall see the root of the bleed without having to undo the whole incision.'

They worked quietly and efficiently,

rather more silent than the television medical dramas suggested. Ian disliked having noisy distractions like pop music playing, though he knew that some of the surgeons found music calmed them.

'Yes, there it is. Nothing major. Just a slight leak round the base of the graft. I should be able to stem it with a suture. He shouldn't be put too far behind in his recovery.'

'His wife will be relieved. Poor soul was in a flat panic.'

'Doubtless you calmed her in your own inimitable way.'

'Hope so,' Matti replied. 'I said I'd go and see her again after the op unless she opted to go home. I did suggest it.'

'What would I do without you?' he said admiringly.

She reacted in her usual predictable way and looked tenderly at the man she loved. *I'll kill Lori if she lets him down,* she vowed silently, wondering once more how she was going to get through the next days. It was going to be an impossible task working closely with him when he totally belonged to someone else. She cursed herself yet again for being so weak as to let it all happen without telling him of her true feelings. She peeled off her theatre gown and mask, dumped them into the basket and left the room.

Matti hadn't made any special plans for the rest of the weekend, assuming she'd be helping Lori with the hundreds of tasks she had been panicking over. Seating plans for the reception, place cards and the special little wedding favours someone had suggested — all of them had to be done at some point. When she had returned from the hospital on Saturday evening, there was no sign of Lori. There was a note on the kitchen counter saying she had gone out. She'd left no details, but at least she had said thank you for the previous evening.

'Great,' Matti muttered. 'Another fun-packed evening with only the television for company. And there's bound to be a medical drama for me to sit and pick holes in.' Ian and Sam would be enjoying the stag night. She wondered what they had planned. Something over-the-top, no doubt, if Sam's reputation was to be believed. She opened the fridge to see if there was anything to eat and found half a bottle of wine. She poured a glass and slumped down onto the sofa. Once Lori moved out, she would have to find a new flatmate. It was too expensive to keep it for just herself and she really needed to get a new sofa. This one was way past being remotely comfortable. Despite this, she fell asleep within five minutes and woke some hours later when it was quite dark. Still no sign of Lori. That girl certainly had stamina, whereas *Matti* was becoming prematurely middle-aged. Once this was all over, she was going to take herself in hand and stop dedicating herself to her career. She was really far too much like Ian in that respect. He was such a dedicated doctor, it was positively freaky the way he'd gone out of character and fallen for Lori. Rebellion or what?

It was too late to eat properly so she made a sandwich and finished the wine. After a long bath she decided to call it a day and went to bed. From the depths of sleep she thought she heard some giggling at around two in the morning but turned over and went back to sleep. She no longer cared what Lori was doing. Ian was surely quite old enough to look after his own interests.

At seven o'clock the next morning she went through to the kitchen, clad only in her short nightie. Slumped on the sofa in the lounge was a male, his feet hanging over the end and his head uncomfortably bent at an angle. The snoring proved it was a living soul and not some corpse lying there. She made her coffee and carried it back, intending to drink it in her room.

'Hmm, nice view. Are there many more of you around here?' The voice was husky and had a definite foreign accent. 'Why don't you come and sit beside me? We should get to know each other.'

'I'm sorry? Who on earth are you and what are you doing on my sofa?'

'I came back with Lori. She's your friend, I guess? Is that coffee? I could use some myself.'

'Kitchen's there. Help yourself.' She stormed into her own room and flung some clothes on. What was Lori thinking of? This sort of thing had happened before, when she'd brought some stray male back, but now things were different. She was getting married this time next week. Quickly flinging on jeans and a baggy T-shirt, she banged on Lori's door.

'Go away,' came a sleepy voice.

'No, I won't go away. There's some man asleep on my sofa. Well, he was asleep until he decided to come on to me. Get up and sort it out.'

'He's harmless. Lovely bloke. You should chat him up. Might be just what you need.'

'You're disgusting. May I remind you

you're getting married next week?'

'Sooo? I need to have a final fling before I settle down to the kitchen sink of life.'

Matti went into her room before she exploded and said something she might regret. How could Lori behave like this when she was about to marry the very best person in the world? Kitchen sink of life? What on earth was that supposed to mean? Did Ian have any idea of what he was taking on? She really needed to put him in the picture, but how could she, without sounding like a total witch? Damned if she did say anything and damned if she didn't. She heard movement and subdued chatter and ventured out to see what was going on. Lori was sitting on the arm of the sofa while whoever-he-was gazed up at her adoringly. They both held coffee mugs (Matti's best ones) in their hands.

'Andreas, you've already met Matti? She's my best friend, a guardian angel.'

'Indeed, we met earlier. And may I

say, I preferred the outfit you were wearing then,' he said in one of the sexiest accents Matti had ever heard. She blushed.

'I had no idea Lori had brought someone back,' she said.

'We were just thinking of going out for brunch somewhere. Fancy joining us?' Lori suggested.

'I thought you had a great deal to do? Getting preparations in hand for next weekend?'

'There's loads of time. Come on. It'll be fun. You worked all day yesterday. You deserve a break.'

'And I'm working all day tomorrow and the next day, so I have loads to do myself. So do you. Or are you expecting me to do everything for this damned wedding of yours?' Andreas raised his black eyebrows.

'Wedding? Whose wedding?'

'Lori's wedding. She's marrying the most gorgeous man on legs next Saturday and she's messing him about.'

'Hey, she never told me about any

wedding. I'm sorry. No wonder you're upset with me. I'll get out of here right away.' He lifted a long body out of his seat and brushed fingers through slightly too long jet-black hair. It was easy to see why Lori had been captivated. 'I'm sorry, Matti. I wouldn't have come back with her if I'd known. Excuse me.' He shot out of the flat as if the hounds of hell were after him.

'Andreas, wait,' Lori called. Matti glared at her. 'Thanks a bunch. I was only having a bit of fun. Something you need in your own life. You'll die a virgin at this rate.'

'How dare you? You have no idea of decency, do you?'

'It's not as if anything happened with Andreas. We both got slightly drunk and he came back here for a coffee. Then he crashed out on the sofa as you saw. I just left him there. And what did you mean about Ian being the most gorgeous man on legs? Is there something I should know?'

'Of course not. Known each other all

our lives. We look out for each other.'
Her cheeks were burning as she turned
away.

'But you'd like it to be much more
than that, wouldn't you?' Lori said
rather spitefully. Her eyes narrowed.
'Yes, I thought so. You're just jealous.
It's nothing to do with how I behave.
You want Ian for yourself, don't you?'

Matti crossed to the window and
looked out, her back to the woman she
had believed was her friend. There was
no point denying it. Why hadn't she
seen what Lori was really like before
now? She really should have said
something much, much sooner.

'I see. I'm right. Well, I am the one
who's in love with him and he feels the
same about me. Like I said, I am just
having my final fling before I'm tied to
one man for life. Don't worry. I intend
to reform once we're married.'

'You'd better. But leopards and spots
spring to mind. I don't actually believe
you love him. You just see him as a
status symbol and you like the idea of

a great big, fancy wedding. Do you really think you're capable of staying with just one man?'

'Even if he is the most gorgeous man on legs?' she repeated with a nasty edge to her voice. 'Okay then, bossy boots. What are all these exciting tasks you think we should be doing? Once I've had some breakfast, of course. Shame I didn't get Andreas's phone number. You might have liked to use it. He clearly liked you.'

'Maybe so. Too late now.'

'Okay then, order of work for today, commandant?'

Matti hesitated. She felt like clearing off out somewhere for the day and leaving Lori to it. But she knew nothing would be done if she left and Lori would undoubtedly find some urgent thing she needed to do that would take her out of the flat for the rest of Sunday.

'You said you had to finalise the seating plan, make up and pack the wedding favours and organise what you needed to take for the honeymoon. Laundry may soon become a priority?'

'Won't need much. I can always pick up some spare tops and things when we're there. Wonder if Ian's got a hangover today? Must say, I think I might have had one tequila too many last night. We went to this fab new place in Newquay.'

'But that's miles away. Hope you didn't drive back?'

'Took a cab. Actually, I was wondering if maybe you'd drive me over to collect my car? We could even go later this evening and make a night of it.'

'No way. But Newquay's seventy miles away. A cab must have cost you a fortune.'

'Andreas paid. Lovely man. Generous with it. Didn't you fancy him just one little bit? He's rather gorgeous really. Greek extraction, but you could probably see that.'

Matti had heard enough. Why should she care any more? If Ian really wanted to marry Lori, then good luck to him. He'd certainly need it.

'You have to be one of the most selfish people I have ever met. You only think of yourself. No I won't drive you to Newquay. Sort out your mistakes yourself.' Lori's lovely face fell and her large green eyes filled with tears. 'Actually,' Matti continued, 'I'm going out. Might even go to see my parents. Good luck with all your wedding plans. You know, I can't wait for you to move out of my flat. Then maybe I can get my life back.'

She stormed out and drove away from the flat and down to a nearby beach. She desperately needed time on her own and despite her words, certainly had no intention of spending the day defending her unhappiness to anyone, let alone her parents. They would immediately know something was wrong and would persist in wringing the truth out of her. What was the truth, though? Lori was what her mother would call *flighty*, but she'd never fully realised just how this flightiness might affect Ian and their marriage.

After sitting in her car for a while to let her anger settle down, she got out and shivered. She grabbed her jacket from the back of the car and stuffed her keys and mobile phone into her jeans, then took a walk along the rocky beach near the sea, where shingle crunched beneath her feet. Her mind was in turmoil. She was torn between wanting to tell Ian the truth and wanting to protect him from being hurt. It was something she would certainly discuss with Sam the next evening. Deep in thought, she became aware of a child screaming. She gave a start and looked round. Someone was running along the beach towards her.

'It's my boy! Look, down there! He's fallen into the water!'

Matti saw the boy, floundering and evidently out of his depth. She ran towards him. He must have slipped off the rocks while trying to catch something in the toy fishing net, now floating rapidly out to sea.

'Rory, hang on! We're coming!' yelled the woman. 'I can't swim! How can I get him out?'

'Have you got a phone? On second thoughts, use mine. Call the coast-guard. Nine, nine, nine. I'll see if I can reach him. There's a bit of a current here so I know I shouldn't dive in. Tell the coastguard you're at the west end of Minley Beach. Do it now.' She was calling instructions to the mother while she was stripping off her shoes and jacket. It was too dangerous to dive in at this point but if she could somehow reach the boy, she might at least drag him to safety. The waves had a huge difference in the rise and fall. Maybe she could use that.

'Here, Rory, try to push yourself towards the rocks. Try to catch my jacket sleeve. See, it's floating towards you. Keep kicking with your legs. Come on. Kick harder.' There was desperation on the little face. He was probably only around eight and was clearly terrified.

'Mummy!' he yelled as he kept bobbing up and down in the waves.

Matti wedged her knee behind a rock and leaned right out as far as she could, tossing her jacket towards the boy. He could almost touch the bottom as the waves came in and out.

'Next time the wave goes out, try to push yourself up as high as you can from the bottom. Great, that's it. Next one, you'll reach my sleeve.' He tried to grab the bright red material as it floated on the water. He missed. 'Never mind, next wave's nearly going back. Big jump this time.'

'Don't worry love, I'll go in after him,' called a male voice behind her.

'Don't you dare. If you get any further out than Rory, you'll be swept away.'

'I can swim all right. Stand by.'

'No!' she bellowed. 'Stay where you are. I've nearly got him. Lie flat beside me and we'll pull him in. Okay, Rory, this is it. Jump.' He did and caught the sleeve between icy cold hands. She rapidly pulled him towards her and managed to catch his wrist. The large man had lain down beside her and he caught the other hand. Together they dragged him to the rocks and managed to lift him out of the water. The child screamed again as his legs were dragged over the rough rocks, lacerating the bare flesh.

'I'm so sorry, love, but we had to get you out before the next waves came and washed all of us off the rocks. It's all right. I'm a nurse. We'll soon get you fixed up.'

'Oh Rory, come here, darling.' His mother caught him in her arms and hugged him. 'You poor little thing, you're freezing.'

'Your jacket's just floated out to sea, love. I can't reach it,' the man told her.

'Not to worry. It did the job.' She shivered, thoroughly chilled by the water that had been washing over her arms and body. 'We need to get him to the hospital to get those cuts sorted.' Rory was sobbing with cold and when he looked down and saw blood pouring out of wounds, he began to scream. 'We need to put something round those legs. Have you got anything with you?'

'We've got a dry towel,' the mother said.

'Okay. Just put it over him very loosely, mostly to keep him warm, but it stops him being frightened. Don't press it tightly or it will stick. And there may be sand in it.' As they walked back to their little encampment, Matti saw that the beach buggy used by the life guards was coming towards them.

'Do you need an ambulance?' called the driver.

'Probably quicker if I drive him myself to hospital. Can you give him a ride back to the car park? Saves us carrying him. Have you got a car?' she asked Rory's mother.

'No. We came by bus and then his dad's coming to fetch us when he finishes work.'

'Okay, well if it's all right with you, we'll drive him to the hospital where I work. Bring your stuff with you and you can phone your husband and tell him where you are. Don't worry. We'll soon have him sorted.' It was lucky she had

43

put her car keys into her jeans or they would be lost, along with her jacket.

A & E was relatively quiet on a Sunday afternoon. Rory had got over the first shock and was now warm in a clean shirt and a jumper.

'Come on then. Let's see what the doctor says about you. Will you come too, Mrs . . . ?'

'It's Mary. Just call me Mary. Would it be all right if I wait here? I'm likely to faint at the sight of so much blood. You'll be all right, won't you, Rory?'

The child was by now quite enjoying the attention and his newly found hero status, not to mention being pushed in a wheelchair. He nodded.

'I'm all right with Matti. She saved me,' he began to tell the doctor.

Soon, the cuts were being washed out and cleaned. There was some sand in the deeper cuts, which caused some anxiety, but Matti managed to keep Rory's attention away from the trickier bits. Soon there were several butterfly strips over the worst cuts and a light covering over his leg to keep it clean.

'So, now tell me how this happened,' the doctor asked.

'I was fishing with my new net. Where's my new net?' he demanded, remembering he hadn't seen it since the accident.

'I'm afraid it went out to sea.'

'Then I slipped and Matti kept telling me to jump and catch her coat. That's gone out to sea as well. I was very clever to catch it, wasn't I?'

'Very clever, darling. Good job you managed to hang on, wasn't it?'

The story was told over and over again to anyone who would listen during the next few minutes, once mother and child were reunited.

'Thank you so much,' Mary said, giving Matti a hug. 'I dread to think what could have happened if you hadn't come along. Oh, and thanks for your phone. How much do I owe you for the calls?'

'Don't be silly. That's fine. Right, well I'll leave you to it.'

She reflected on her day. If she hadn't stormed out of the flat that morning, that child could well have drowned. Fate was obviously at work. Despite her rather scruffy and soggy state, she decided to go to the cardiac unit and see how Mr Palmer was faring. She went into the office and called up the name on the computer. Records were always constantly monitored and she could access the details from the office machine. All was well. That was a relief. Poor Mrs Palmer was elderly herself and clearly wouldn't easily cope if anything had gone wrong. She flicked through the other patients she had been dealing with and saw that all was well. One had already been moved into HDU, leaving a bed vacant for tomorrow's new batch.

'Bit like a production line, isn't it?' said a voice behind her.

'Ian? What are you doing here? I thought you'd be nursing a hangover.'

'You know me. I hate having a hangover. I doubt Sam is quite so clear-headed, however. He kindly finished every drink I turned down. But it was a good night. We enjoyed ourselves. Had some laughs. So, what's new with you? Thought you were planning to be knee-deep in wedding stuff all day?' She looked away from him, wondering what on earth she could say.

'Change of plan. I decided I needed some air and left Lori to her own devices. I went to the beach where there was a bit of a drama with a kid. Had to be fished out of the sea. Then I thought I'd come and check on our charges.'

'How typical of you. You get a day off and choose to come in to see how the patients are doing. And help some stray kid into the bargain. You're just too good to everyone, Matti. But you do look a bit bedraggled. And you're shivering. Let's go and have a coffee or something. Come on. You look in need of it and one of your favourite double chocolate chip something-or-others.'

She allowed herself to be led down to the canteen, where she sat at a side table waiting for her knight in shining armour to deliver coffee and cake.

'You're remarkable, you know. You stuff these vast muffins down and never show an ounce of fat anywhere.' He put the tray down and flopped down beside her. 'This won't stop once I'm married, will it?'

'What do you mean?'

'We'll still share coffees and things and still be best friends, won't we?'

She gave a snort. 'I hope so. Though Lori won't like it if you spend too much time with me.'

'Don't be daft. We're working together all the time, aren't we? Our shifts always coincide and we have meal breaks at the same time. And we even manage to find each other on our day off.' He paused and looked at her with his special smile. 'Besides, I need you in my life, to tell me what to do.' He caught her hand and pressed her fingers to his lips. 'I love you Matti, you know I do.'

So why are you marrying Lori? her inner voice screamed. She felt the old

48

sensation of tears blowing up inside and struggled to contain them. *You shouldn't be marrying her; you should be marrying me. She's a flirt and she'll break your heart. She'll undoubtedly be unfaithful in a very short time. She can't help herself.* It would have been all too easy to say it out loud.

'So, are we still friends?'

'Of course,' she managed to mumble. 'Just don't expect everything to stay just the same. You'll have new interests and new things to do as you make your lives together. I'm not going to be a part of any of that, am I now?' Her words nearly choked her. What did he mean by 'love'? She loved *him* with all her heart. It had only become this clear since he and Lori were engaged. Why didn't he see it? Her whole body longed for real love from this man . . . for the whole package of love, marriage, and even a family. Her thoughts were dragged back to reality.

'And what about you?' he asked, perhaps a little wistfully. 'Will you get a new flatmate? And what about boy-friends? Is there someone new on the scene?' There was an edge to his voice, she was sure. She shook her head. 'So, we can stay best friends?'

'Of course we'll always be friends. How could we not be?'

She concentrated on her muffin and sipped the coffee, wishing she could be less aware of his dark grey eyes that shone with silvery lights. His presence almost overwhelmed her. She had never wanted anyone this much. It had only become so very obvious to her since he had become engaged to someone else. Why did she keep up her stupid damned loyalty to a flatmate she was now actually growing to dislike? Per-haps it was just jealousy after all and she needed to push these thoughts away. Somehow she had to cope with the business of being a friend and chief bridesmaid. For two pins she'd turn that job down right now if she could.

3

Sunday evening at the flat was tense. Lori had clearly done some thinking during the day instead of collecting her car.

'I'm so sorry, Matti. I was being a cow this morning. Put it down to pre-nuptial nerves and the hangover from hell. I know Saturday night was a big mistake. I hold up my hands. I'm going to get a train to Newquay tomorrow to collect my car. I've got the whole week off, thank heavens. Well, once tomorrow's night shift is done, at least. Plenty of time to get all the last-minute stuff sorted. I have a wedding dress fitting on Tuesday morning and the rest of the week's my own. I'll sort all this wedding paraphernalia then. Okay?'

'A dress fitting after an all-night shift? You'll be dead on your feet.'

'Can't help it. I needed to make the appointment early in the week in case there are any changes needed. So, am I forgiven for being a stupid cow?'

Matti shrugged, knowing she couldn't speak the truth. She didn't have the right words in her vocabulary.

'So how were the parents?' Lori asked her.

'Oh, I didn't make it to them. I stopped at the beach and got involved in helping in an accident. Once a nurse, always a nurse, you know.'

'You're well in line for a sainthood, Matti. Amazing nurse. Saving lives all over the place. No wonder Ian talks about you all the time.'

'He does? Really? But he loves you, doesn't he?'

'Yes indeedy. I'm a lucky girl.'

Matti could have slapped her smug face but resisted the temptation. It wasn't the sort of thing she did, was it? 'I'll start on supper, shall I?'

'All done. There's a chicken thing in the oven.'

'Oh, really? Great. I can't smell anything though.'

'Damn. I forgot to switch it on. What am I like? Okay, don't tell me. Rhetorical question.'

There was no sign of the various wedding things she had been planning to do and Matti was determined not to mention it again. They sat watching some television documentary until she decided an early night was needed. This was the last night she was going to spend like this, she vowed. If everyone thought she was a martyr, she would make things happen to prove them wrong.

★ ★ ★

'I'd like you sit in on my clinic this afternoon,' Ian invited her the next morning.

'Is that all right? I mean, doesn't your registrar usually do it?'

'He's off sick. I like the way you reassure nervous patients. Besides, you must know nearly as much as I do about heart surgery after all this time.'

'Huh, I don't think so. But thanks for the compliment. I'd be pleased to sit in with you. So, what have we got this morning?'

'Another CABG. Double, I think.' CABG was the shorthand they used for a coronary artery bypass graft. 'Not that one, two, three or four replacements make a lot of difference once the patient is opened up. How's life at the flat, by the way? Lori working hard?'

'She's got her last shift tonight. Haven't you spoken to her?'

'I did call yesterday but there was no reply. I'll try her later.' Matti stared at him. Lori had been in all day, according to her story. Why hadn't she answered her phone? Did Ian have a bit of a strained look about the eyes? In fact, he was generally looking rather weary.

'Are you all right? You look tired.'

'Haven't been sleeping too well. Expect it's something to do with this impending wedding.' Matti pursed her lips but said nothing.

'Shall I go and check the patient has had the pre-med and is ready to go down?'

'Thanks.'

The ward was busy with new patients arriving and anxious families waiting in the small lounge area for beds to become available. Patients were being moved from HDU into the separate small wards of four beds. Once here, the caregiving was less intense and patients were worked hard with the physios in attendance.

'You've got a patient ready for us?' she asked at the nursing station.

'Oh yes, bay G. Mrs Howorth. She's had the pre-med but she's still just about with us.'

'Thanks. I'll have a word and then I think we'll be ready for her in theatre.' She went into bay G and said good morning to the patient.

'Hallo, Doctor. This is it then.'

'I'm not actually your doctor but I shall be with you in theatre. I'm Sister

Harper. Anything else you need to ask before we go down?'

'It will be all right, won't it? I mean, I am going to wake up back here, aren't I?'

'You won't actually be here. Remember what the doctor told you? You'll be in the intensive . . . special care ward where there are lots of people to look after you. There will be a lot of machines, computers and monitors and such all round but they're all there to look after you. Nothing to be afraid of. And of course, our Mr Faulkner is one of the very best surgeons in the country.' She took the lady's hand and held it, as the porters arrived to wheel her bed along to the theatre.

Ian was already gowned and greeted his patient. 'Morning, Mrs Howorth. We're going to put you to sleep now and see what we can do to help you feel better.'

The anaesthetist stepped forward and told her to begin counting down. She reached four before she was asleep.

'Okay, ready,' the anaesthetist said.

A different registrar was assisting Ian as his usual partner was away. Matti worked as professionally as ever, stepping forward with the different implements as necessary. It always amazed her that this procedure could be done so easily and that such hugely invasive surgery actually repaired itself so quickly afterwards. There was no denying that it was a major operation, but the wonderful surgeons managed the whole thing so calmly. With intense concentration, the operation was completed. Everything had gone in the usual textbook style of Ian's operations. 'Matter of plumbing really,' was Ian's usual comment, though they all knew it was much more than that.

'I think we're done here. Thanks, everyone. Good job.'

'Been a pleasure to work with you, Mr Faulkner. If ever you have a vacancy on your team, please bear me in mind,' the stand-in registrar said.

'Thanks, I will.'

Matti began to collect the implements while the other theatre staff cleared and cleaned the rest of the room. One of the other cardiac teams would be using the theatre during the afternoon. It was indeed something of a production line. She went to the preparation room and took off her gown. She was just in time to see Ian's well-formed torso as he stripped off his top. He put on clean scrubs and smiled at her.

'Sorry. Didn't realise you were there. But there's nothing you haven't seen before.'

'Course not,' she hissed. She'd come within an inch of touching his bare back, just to feel his skin against her hand.

He would check on his patient in intensive care later, before he began the afternoon clinic. There were always long queues of patients awaiting this surgery and Ian managed to treat them all with dedication and courtesy, as if they were the only ones undergoing the procedure. Yet one more reason Matti could love and admire the man who was so good at his job.

She collected sandwiches and coffee from the canteen and took them along to Ian's office. It was their usual routine on operating and clinic days. Ian was busily writing up the paperwork for the morning's operation and once completed, he opened the stack of files to look through the afternoon list.

'Come on, eat something and take a break.'

'Thanks. Haven't got time but I can munch while I read. Darn it, I meant to call Lori but haven't had a minute.'

'I'll leave you to it if you want to call her now.'

'It's OK. Stay where you are. I only want to check she's all right. I haven't seen her for a few days, with one thing and another.' He picked up the phone and dialled her mobile.

Matti's mobile rang at the same time. She went out of the office and answered it in the passage. It was Sam, Doctor Grayling.

'Hi Matti. Are we still on for dinner this evening?'

'Oh yes, of course,' Matti replied. She'd almost forgotten about the date, if date it really was.

'Great. I'll pick you up at seven, if you give me your address. Then we can dish the dirt on the prospective bride and groom and get to know each other a little along the way. Oh, and don't let anything Ian says put you off me. I am very reliable and not nearly the womaniser he'd have you think.'

'Don't disappoint me,' she joked. Matti gave him the address and switched off her phone. She frowned as she remembered the things she had planned to discuss with Sam. It wasn't really going to be a fun evening at all. In fact, she wondered if it was right to say anything at all about her concerns. After all, Lori was supposed to be her friend, despite everything. She peered through the window in Ian's door to check whether he was still on the phone but he was back to reading his notes. His dark head was bent over the patient notes and he wrote his own queries in his favourite green

60

pen. At least you always knew which were Ian's notes in the distinctive colour, she thought fondly.

'All well with you?' she asked.

'I guess so. Did Lori say anything to you about her plans for today?'

'Not really. Why?'

'She's not answering either the flat number or her mobile. If I was the suspicious type, I'd almost wonder if she was trying to avoid me.'

'Oh she was going to . . . ' Matti remembered with a start that Lori planned to go and retrieve her car all the way from Newquay. There was no way she could tell Ian that little snippet of information as he would demand an explanation for why the car was in Newquay in the first place. 'She's probably still out shopping. I'm sure she has heaps to do.'

'But if she has an all-night shift tonight, she ought to be getting some sleep. She really does need taking in hand. She doesn't take enough care of her health.'

Matti gave a shrug. 'Who could ever tell Lori what to do?'

'Meaning?' Ian looked perturbed.

'Nothing. She's just a law unto herself.'

'You sound edgy.' He stared at her, waiting for her to say more, but she gave a shrug and looked away. 'I suppose we'd better get started on this clinic. With any luck, I might get away in time to catch Lori before she leaves for her shift.'

There were a large number of appointments — people coming for their pre-admission checks and others for consultations to decide on their treatment. They had been referred here by the regional hospitals and all wanted reassurance.

'I don't really understand what a bypass is,' one of the patients announced. Ian smiled, inwardly cursing, as his was really the final stage when all the explanations should have been completed by the teams examining the patient earlier on.

'Well, it means that your arteries

carrying the blood from your heart have become blocked. A bit like a blocked pipe stops the water flowing around the house. We have to find another way to let it flow and so we put in a new artery which works as a bypass to carry the blood to where it needs to be. Once it's begun to heal, you will feel much better. The shortness of breath will go and the pains you've been experiencing will disappear.'

'I see. Thank you, Doctor. And where do you get the new artery from?'

'We take a piece of vein from your leg. One that isn't too important and that you can manage without.'

The consultation went on and eventually the patient was satisfied.

'If you'd like to come with me, I'll show you where you need to go next,' Matti told him.

'Thank you, Nurse. I s'pose you are a nurse?'

'Yes, I am. Come along now. I'll give you some leaflets to look through and you can ask your own doctor if there's anything else you want to know.' She ushered him out, despite his unwillingness to leave. Ian shot her a grateful look and pushed the papers into the file and took out the next one.

'I'm just a glorified plumber,' he muttered, 'working on a production line.'

Matti tried to find time to answer many of the patients' questions, particularly when she took them back to the waiting area. They usually asked about things they hadn't liked to 'bother the doctor with'. Patiently, she would explain things in a simple way so they felt reassured. Each time she was able to tell them that Mr Faulkner was one of the very best surgeons in the country.

'Why do you call him 'Mister' when he's a doctor?' one of them asked.

'It's traditional to say 'Mister' when he's a consultant and a surgeon. Shows they have certain qualifications.'

'I see. So he's still a doctor, is he? I mean, he's had the training?'

'Oh yes, of course. He's had a lot of extra specialist training besides.'

By four-thirty, the last patient was shown out.

'Thanks so much. You did a great job,' Ian told her.

'My pleasure. I enjoyed it. I just hope I was useful. I thought I'd go up and see Mrs Howorth.'

'No need. I was going myself, and then I think we can safely call it a day. We've two more tomorrow, though I think one is a valve replacement, if my memory serves me correctly. Anyway, come along with me if you like. I'm sure Mrs H will be pleased to see a friendly face.'

As always, it felt good to be working so closely with him and to know that he clearly relied on her and respected what she did. Not that any of it could help her private feelings. Maybe he knew of an operation for this sort of broken heart? But she thought she was holding things together very well under the circumstances. Once Saturday was over, things would have to change, but they would surely find a new way of working together.

'So, where's Sam taking you tonight?'

'Not sure. He's picking me up from the flat.'

'It'll probably be one of his favourite pubs with a lot of loud music. He's a folk music fanatic and always knows when and where there's a session.'

'Doesn't sound conducive to much discussion but I expect it'll be fine.'

'Don't let him lead you astray.' He smiled. 'He's always a bit of a joker and not to be taken too seriously.'

'Does he have a girlfriend?'

'Several. He hates the thought of settling down with just one. I keep telling him it's only a matter of time till he meets the right one. Hey, maybe it could be you. What do you think?'

'No way. I suspect any Mr Right is non-existent for me.'

He stared at her. 'I don't know what you mean. You're gorgeous. You have a perfect figure and lovely hair. You're intelligent. Good company and a very talented nurse.' She blushed a deep scarlet and found her tongue had somehow glued itself to the roof of her mouth so couldn't speak. 'Sorry, I have clearly embarrassed you. Dear Matti. If I wasn't already committed, I'd marry you tomorrow.'

'Shame. I'm busy tomorrow, remember? Operations? Gotta go now,' she squeaked. Her heart was pounding out of control and if she didn't remove herself from this man right away, she would definitely be the one needing that heart surgery. How could he say that? She had been around for him most of their adult lives but just when he felt safe with someone else, he could think about offering everything she once wanted. Still wanted, damn it.

'Matti? What is it?' she heard him call after her. She had to get right away. She didn't want to be at the flat tonight when he called to see Lori. She would go to the cinema or something. But that was no good. Sam was coming to collect her. Damn, damn, damn.

Ian watched as she raced along the corridor and out of his sight. What had he said to upset her so much? He thought over his words. He had intended to compliment her. To tell how her how lovely she was and how much he cared. He stopped. Could it really be that Matti . . . ? No. Impossible. They were like brother and sister. Weren't they? He'd always thought the world of Matti. Maybe they were just too close and so he'd never considered a romantic involvement with her. But had he ever asked her about her feelings? Had he ever thought of her as more than a very special friend? He'd always been concentrating on his career. Too busy to think about having any sort of relationship with anyone. Then Lori had bounced into his life and taken him over. He'd been totally captivated by the lovely, lively Lori when she'd arrived on the scene. Was it really only six or seven weeks ago? She had flirted with him unashamedly.

She made him feel special and really alive for the first time in years, dragging him out to discos and clubs and introducing him to different music. She had laughed when he asked her to marry him. Actually, had he asked her or had she asked him? Hadn't she said something about her life plan being to marry an eminent surgeon? He tried to recall her words at the time.

'My dream wedding . . . ' She had closed her eyes in a dreamy way. 'I want the full white frothy stuff and hordes of guests sipping obscene quantities of champagne. Oh, yes please. Let's get married as soon as we can. Sounds like just what I need. And you an eminent surgeon to boot. What more could a lowly nurse want?' On reflection, it sounded as if she just wanted the whole wedding scene and he happened to be there with the right qualifications.

He reflected on her words. Whenever he asked her if she really loved him, she'd always said, 'Of course I do. Madly, darling.' Hardly a sincere-sounding response.

Was she marrying a status symbol or a real person? But then, who wouldn't fall for someone like Lori? All the same, in the few weeks they'd known each other, just how many evenings had they spent together? And did he really enjoy the various clubs she had dragged him to? He'd never admitted to her that it wasn't really his thing but because it made her happy, he'd gone along with her demands. He could just about tolerate Sam's taste for folk clubs but he preferred classical music, the sort of concerts he and Matti had gone to together at university. He and Matti really did have more in common than his bride-to-be.

'It's all just wedding nerves,' he muttered out loud as he arrived at the ITU. He was clearly suffering from the dreaded pre-wedding doubts that everyone talked about. Of course he loved Lori. Didn't everyone? He'd call Sam and hopefully his friend would soon settle his nerves. Only, Sam was going out with Matti that evening. He didn't much like that idea. Sam was a great friend, but would he treat Matti properly? Why should he feel so concerned about this wedding? Was he making the biggest mistake of his life? Perhaps he was simply making some breakout statement, a rebellion? He had spent far too many years perfecting his skills as a surgeon and his social life had been passing him by. Was Lori just some sort of rebellion he'd thought he needed? Only a few days to go and he would be committed for life. Was Lori truly making the same commitment? As for Matti, he realised that he had probably taken her for granted for much too long.

4

'Oh Sam, you're such a fool. I haven't laughed so much in ages.' Matti had enjoyed their meal far more than she had expected.

'Glad to hear it. I'm usually known as the village idiot. Now, I understand you have a chocolate addiction?'

'Erm, yes. I suppose Ian passed on that snippet of information?'

'Actually it was Dolores in the canteen. She said they have to order extra supplies of chocolate muffins whenever you're on duty. They get a special issue of the staff rota so they know in good time.'

'What? Really? Dolores? Who's she?'

'Okay, it was Ian. Ordered me to ensure I took you to a place to eat that provided puddings with extra chocolate. There's a marvellous monster pudding on the menu. One for us to share, if that's okay with you?'

'Sounds good to me.' She giggled at his words. Dolores indeed.

He went to the bar and ordered it and came back to their table looking serious. 'I don't want to put a blanket on this delightful evening but I think we need to talk seriously for a minute. I have some concerns about this forthcoming marriage and wondered if we could put cards on the table?' he said.

'I'd like that. I'm really worried too. You go first.'

'Okay. You know Lori better than I do but I always get the feeling she's playing some sort of game. I can totally understand Ian falling for her. She's fun, lively and of course, totally gorgeous. And completely not Ian's type.'

'So what is Ian's type?'

'Do you really need to ask?' Sam gave her a rueful smile. She stared at him, wondering if he had guessed the truth about her feelings. 'You've known him most of his life, I gather. And you know Lori.'

'You know, I'm not sure I do. I've really only known her a short time. She moved into my flat to share about three months ago. I actually introduced them when Ian came round for a meal one night. He's always come for the odd meal with me for years. She latched onto him and before I knew it, she announced they were engaged.'

'I don't think they've even spent a great deal of time together, have they?' Matti gave a shrug. 'Our Ian is something of an innocent where women are concerned. He always took medical school much too seriously, as far as I can gather. He was always very ambitious. Well, let's face it, you don't get to be a top cardiac surgeon at thirty-one if you don't work for it. But as for Lori. Well, do you really think he knows what he's doing? Have they spent proper quality time together?'

'I don't know to be honest. Lori rarely shared her social calendar with me. I just assumed they were together when she went out and didn't come home. Look, there is something I should to tell you. She went to a club on Saturday and picked up some bloke. She brought him back to the flat. I was furious and even he was pretty upset when he learned she was getting married. Typical I guess. Said it was her final fling before Saturday. Admittedly he slept on the sofa as far as I know.' Sam's face was a picture of shock. He was quiet and couldn't speak for a while. 'Sorry. Maybe I shouldn't have said anything but I just don't know what to do.'

'Of course you needed to say something to someone. I really think we have to say something to Ian too. I doubt he'd listen though. Oh what a mess. I have to admit, she did try to come on to me once, too. She was working in my department at the time and tried to persuade me to go to some club with her. I said that sort of club wasn't my thing and she looked most put out. That was just before the engagement. Look, I know we're both good friends of Ian's. We want to do the best for him, don't we?'

'Oh Sam, I don't know how to say anything without sounding as if I'm jealous. It just sounds nasty if I say anything, but I really don't want him to make a huge mistake. I'd give anything to make him see the reality of it all.'

'Don't worry, I'll try to find a way of warning him. Now, this looks like our pudding arriving.'

The waitress brought a large glass bowl filled with a chocolate mousse, garnished with a selection of fresh fruit and topped with cream. The whole was sprinkled with chocolate flakes.

'Oh wow. This looks like a whole month's chocolate fix in one fell swoop. A heart attack in a bowl. Amazing.' For several moments they were both silent as they dipped spoons into the concoction. 'This is heaven,' Matti murmured at last, her eyes closed.

'Don't turn round now but you'll never guess who's just come in.'

'Who?'

'Lori and some bloke.'

'But she's doing a night shift tonight. Her last one before the wedding.'

'She doesn't exactly look like a nurse on night shift duty to me. It's okay, they're going into the other dining room. I think she may have seen us but she's not coming over.'

'I don't understand. Who is she with? And what is she doing here when she should be on duty?'

'Good-looking bloke, whoever he is. Youngish and obviously knows her well.' They finished their meal and decided to leave. Matti felt sick at heart and wanted to leave without having to face Lori.

'Come back to my flat for coffee and we'll decide what we should do next,' she suggested. 'Try to find a strategy for putting Ian into the true picture.'

They drove back in silence, both busy with their own thoughts. If Lori was about to have a meal with someone, she wouldn't be back for some time, so she and Sam could talk undisturbed.

She made a pot of coffee and brought it into the living room.

'So, what are we going to do? Perhaps we shouldn't tell Ian the truth. Let him discover it for himself.' Matti felt tears pricking her eyes and knew she didn't want Ian to be punished.

'Hey, come on. You know that isn't the right thing to do.' He moved to sit next to her and put his arms round her shoulders. 'Don't be upset.' He leaned forward and lifted her chin and kissed her gently. He pulled her closer and kissed her again. 'Look, I know you really care about Ian but you mustn't let it destroy your life. I do think he's a fool. He's spent far too much time working and hardly ever enjoying himself and Lori has just swept him along with her enjoyment of life. She's pushed him into it. He hasn't thought it through and has snatched at this chance in case he misses out. More fool him. If she was likely to go off with someone else, her feelings couldn't have been very sincere in the first place.'

'I know you're right. I just wish I'd said something sooner. But in all truth, I didn't realise what Lori was really like until very recently and nor did I realise how deeply I felt about Ian, until it was too late.'

'You mean . . . you and Ian?' He moved away and stared at her. 'You actually love Ian? And here's me thinking *we* were getting on really well.' He pulled a mock sad face. 'I thought I might stand a chance. You know what they say about the best man and chief bridesmaid? I'd made secret plans to whisk you away somewhere as soon as the ceremonials were over.' He was grinning and she wasn't sure whether to believe him or not.

'Oh Sam, you're so nice. But it's no use. I can't feel anything real for anyone. Not at this point in time.'

'How sad all round. I suppose I'd better remove my arm from round your shoulders in that case. Pity. I was getting to like it there.' She gave him a hug and kissed his cheek.

'You're a great guy. Give me some time and who knows? I have to get out of this stupid rut I'm in. I'm working on it. But, thank you for being so understanding. Now, how about that coffee?'

The doorbell rang and she raised her eyebrows.

'Who on earth is that, at this time of night? Excuse me.' She returned with a look of surprise on her face. 'Look who I've found on the doorstep.'

'Ian? What are you doing here?' Sam asked.

'I wondered if I could see Lori? I've been trying to contact her all day and all evening but she hasn't replied. I even went to the hospital in the end to catch her on duty but she's not there. She phoned in sick, apparently.'

'She isn't here,' Matti replied. 'Perhaps she's feeling better now and she's gone in late.' She gave a wry smile. Phoned in sick? Lori was out with someone else having a meal. She looked at Sam, wondering who should say something first.

'I've just come from the hospital. Didn't you see her when you got in from work?'

'No. I assumed she'd gone to start her shift early. We're just having coffee. Do you want some?'

'No. I'll go out and look for her. She may have had an accident or something.' He turned and rushed out before they could stop him.

'Ian, hold on mate,' Sam called after him. But his friend ignored him and rushed off. 'Damnation. We should have told him the truth. I'll have to try to catch him tomorrow. Have lunch or something.'

'You'll be lucky. We're operating again tomorrow. All day. You might catch him at night. I can't possibly say anything, not when we're operating. It wouldn't be fair. He needs to focus and doesn't want his mind on other things. He doesn't finish working at the hospital till Thursday. He's booked in loads of patients, wanting to clear the decks before he goes away.'

'Typical Ian. Maybe I can drag him out tomorrow evening. Maybe we should all go together? Unless he plans to spend the time with Lori. Don't worry, Matti. We'll do our best to sort things out.' He stood up to leave. Again, he pulled Matti into a rather comforting hug and kissed her cheek. 'You sure I don't stand a chance?'

She smiled at him again. 'You're a lovely man. Give me time. Let's see what happens. Besides, why me? Ian says you have dozens of girlfriends.'

'I wish. There's nobody special. Maybe it's just that I've been waiting for the right one to come along. You've got something though. You are the right girl for Ian. I don't know why he hasn't seen it before now. Night.'

'Night, and thank you for a lovely meal and mostly, a very enjoyable evening.'

He left and she watched him drive away. His words had done little to comfort her and she felt a deep despair beginning to creep over her. Sadly, she dumped the coffee things in the sink and decided to go to bed before she had to face Lori.

Despite her vow to stop being a martyr, that black despair was all too present. Sleep was a long time coming and she worried that she would be wrecked the next day. The more she tried to nod off, the more difficult it was. She kept listening for Lori to come in, despite not wanting to see her, but she heard nothing. She looked into Lori's room early next morning but her bed hadn't been slept in. Maybe she'd really had some sort of accident but somehow, she doubted it. With a heavy heart, she got ready for work and having to face Ian. At least she had now shared some of her concerns with Sam, and that felt marginally better, but her worst fears seemed to have been confirmed.

'Have you seen her?' was Ian's first question next morning.

'Well, no. But she had today off anyway. Dress fitting I think. Now, have we got today's list yet?' Matti wanted desperately to hide the truth from him.

It may have been cowardly but they had a hectic day ahead and they both really needed to be able to concentrate.

'Yes, of course. We've got the list. But I'm out of my mind with worry about Lori. What on earth can have happened to her?'

'I expect she went somewhere and felt unable to drive for some reason and stayed over with a friend.'

'You mean she didn't go home last night? I thought you just meant you'd left her asleep.'

Matti bit her lip. She should have pretended she didn't know, but it was too late now. He stared at her as if looking could provide him with answers.

'I suppose we'd better prepare for the day,' he said decisively. 'Can't let the patients down.'

'Shall I get you a coffee?' she offered. It was usually his routine before they began work.

'I'm fine. Let's get started. Sooner we start, the sooner we shall finish. Then I can see this girl I'm supposed to be marrying and find out exactly what's going on.' Matti said nothing. She couldn't trust herself to speak. He grimaced slightly and asked, 'So, how was your evening with Sam?'

'Fine, thanks.' They were walking to the theatre as he spoke so there was little time for a proper conversation. 'He's really nice. I've only seen him around before. Never spoken to him much. You've known him long?'

'Ages. Worked together for a long time during training. Before we went off into different specialities. Then we met up again here. Played squash. Usual stuff. He's a good bloke as well as a good doctor. Very dedicated.'

'That's what he says about you.'

'Oh, so you discussed me, did you?'

'Of course. Why else do you think we went out?'

'You will take care, Matti, won't you? I don't want you getting hurt.'

'Why should I be hurt by Sam? He's a lovely guy but not really my type. All the same, I'll be glad to have him standing beside me at the wedding,' she said, feeling the familiar lump growing in her throat. She pushed open the theatre doors, managing to cover the slight quaver she felt in her voice.

The first operation went like clockwork and the bypass graft was completed in record time. As always, Ian thanked the theatre staff and went into the changing area to strip off.

'If you're okay to continue, we'll take a late lunch and have the next one in right away. Shouldn't be complicated. The angiogram suggested a double would be necessary. I'd like to finish as early as possible this afternoon.'

'Fine by me. After my enormous dinner last night, I'm hardly going to faint with hunger.'

'Good. I got someone to phone the ward to prep Mr King early.'

It was unusual to see Ian quite so stressed. A couple of times, she pushed things into his hand when his mind wandered slightly and he slowed down. The theatre phone rang a couple of times and he looked up hopefully, though everyone, even Lori, knew it was bad form to call for anything less than a dire emergency during an operation. He even forgot to thank everyone in his usual way at the end and he left the theatre without a word.

'What's up with him?' the anaesthetist asked.

'He's getting married in a couple of days. Can affect even him, it seems,' one of the nurses said.

'Poor bloke. She'll take some keeping up with, that one,' the anaesthetist added. 'Sorry, Matti. Lori's a friend of yours, isn't she?'

'Shares my flat for another couple of days, at least. What do you mean, anyway?'

'She went out with a friend of mine for a while but she was never still for two minutes. Always wanting to buy something or go somewhere else. He'd had enough of her after a bit. Glad to move on. Has Ian known her long?'

'Not really. But as they say, why wait,

when you find what you want. Excuse me now. I need to get on.'

She went back to Ian's office to help with the post-operation notes, as usual. He was on the phone and she went out again, in case he was talking to Lori. He waved her inside.

'It was Sam. He's suggested we go out, the three of us, this evening. Okay with you? Says there are things he'd like to discuss. Do you know what's troubling him?'

She gave a shrug. 'Wedding stuff I s'pose. Logistics. Did you catch Lori?'

'No. She's just not answering either the phone at the flat or her mobile. I've left messages everywhere. I'll finish up here and get home. Maybe I'll catch her somewhere along the way. Tell her to call me, if you see her, won't you?'

'Course I will. Where are we going this evening?'

'Said we'd meet at the Victory, seven-thirty, if that's all right with you?'

'Fine.'

'Thought we'd have a pasty or

something. Save getting anything to eat at home.'

They finished their work, checked the day's patients, and Ian went off. Matti faced the evening with some trepidation. She looked forward to spending time with the two men in some ways, but knowing the subjects they had to cover and the truths they needed to impart made it worrying.

Lori was in the bath when Matti arrived home. She was singing along to the radio, sounding as if she hadn't a care in the world. Matti made some coffee and sat with her feet up, trying to relax. When her flatmate finally emerged from the bathroom, she behaved as if nothing had happened since they had last met.

'So, how was your last shift?' Matti asked innocently.

'Nothing special.'

'Busy?'

'Not bad.'

'Don't lie to me. You phoned in sick. Then you went out to dinner with yet another man.'

'How did you . . . ?'

'I saw you. We saw you. Sam and I were eating in the same restaurant. Evidently you didn't notice us. And Ian has been frantically trying to contact you all day.'

'Oh. Sorry. I lost my mobile phone.'

'He left messages here too. Didn't you check?'

'Sorry again. Had stuff on my mind.'

'Did you go to your dress fitting?'

'It's tomorrow.'

'You changed it?'

'Er no. It's tomorrow.'

'Lori, you're totally hopeless. It was today, Tuesday. So the dressmaker had time to alter it if necessary and finally finish the hem. Don't you remember? She said she always does the hem at the last fitting to allow for any changes. Shoes and all that.'

'I'll go tomorrow.'

'You hope. She may have someone else booked in tomorrow. Oh, Lori. I'm going to go and get my shower now. I'm out this evening.'

'Get you. Two nights on the trot. I'm out myself. I'm going out with Ian. Last planning meeting before D-Day.'

'Does Ian know?'

'Not yet. I'll phone him later.'

'Only I'm supposed to be going out with him and Sam. We have things to discuss.'

'Sorry. You'll have to wait. I always come first with him.'

'So, this chap last night? Who was he?'

'Oh my, er, my cousin. Flew in from the States. I had to spend time with him, didn't I?'

'Including the night?'

'I crashed at his place. We were late finishing the meal so it made sense.'

'His place, being?'

'He's got a flat just outside Plymouth.'

'Keeps it all the time he's away, does he?'

'What are you getting at? Look, is there something you want to say to me?'

'I simply don't know how you can

behave the way you do. You're supposed to be marrying a wonderful man in a few days and here you are out with other men all the time and paying no attention to Ian at all.'

'I told you, Davo is a cousin. And I'm seeing Ian tonight. Good enough for you? Now, if you don't mind, leave me in private to call my fiancé. Don't worry, after this weekend you'll be rid of me. No more worries about how I behave and you can start your life over again, with Ian out of your hair and heart for good.'

Unable to speak, Matti left her to her call. She wondered if she should call Sam and tell him their plans had once more fallen victim to Lori's whims. Undoubtedly, Ian would prefer to go out with her rather than listen to their fears and worries. She called Sam on her mobile and told him of Lori's demands to see Ian that evening.

'Let's go out anyway. Better than you sitting moping on your own. Pint and a pasty sounds like some sort of therapy, don't you think?'

'Okay, thanks. I must admit, I'd probably do something drastic if I stay in. Chuck all Lori's clothes in the bin and . . . well, generally rubbish most of her possessions.'

'Go Matti!' he replied.

The pub was crowded but they managed to find a corner seat. As predicted, Ian had accepted Lori's invitation — or was it a demand? Sam was angry with his friend but there was little he could do about it. Lori had flicked her fingers and Ian had gone running. Matti told Sam of her conversation with Lori about the previous evening.

'He was supposed to be a cousin, newly arrived from America.'

He laughed. 'They were a bit clingy for cousins. Besides, I was certain she had seen us.'

'Apparently not. Maybe she preferred not to see us, even if she did. Wow, I'm getting thoroughly nasty, aren't I?'

'Look, I've been thinking things over. You're in an awful position, working with Ian all the time. I heard about your heroics on the beach the other day and how well you dealt with the kid involved. My department could use a skilled theatre sister, and someone who's so good with kids would be a huge asset. How about moving to paediatrics? Then at least you wouldn't have to be on top of a situation that you hated.'

'Oh Sam, that's very good of you. But I love cardiac surgery, and working with Ian is really great. Personal issues aside, of course. Is there really a vacancy in your department though?'

'Certainly is. I'd be delighted to work with you. I think we'd make a splendid team and you'd be able to start again.'

'Thanks. I'll certainly give it some thought. Anyway, what are we going to do about this man of ours?'

5

Sam and Matti talked for much of the evening, finding all manner of subjects to interest them but always coming back to Ian and Lori. They finally agreed that Sam would catch Ian the next day, for lunch at the very least. With only three days to go before the wedding, time was getting very short.

'You do see why it can't be me telling Ian about Lori's behaviour? I don't like leaving it to you but anything I say really does look like sour grapes.'

As they parted, Sam once more urged her to think about changing departments. She agreed to think about it but knew that it would not be a sensible career move. When she returned to the flat, she was surprised to find Lori already back from her evening out.

'Ian was in a funny mood. Have you

been saying something to him?' she accused Matti.

'Not really. I did let slip that you hadn't come home last night. Didn't mean to but it sort of came out.'

'Thanks a bunch. Where does loyalty come into this?'

'Loyalty to whom?'

'Me of course. You're my chief bridesmaid, aren't you?'

'Maybe I should resign.'

'Oh Matti, you can't. There's far too much to do. Things have got out of hand and I've got a million things to do. And now I've got to get a new mobile as well. Thought I'd get one of those clever ones that do emails and everything. What do you think?'

'Have you got that sort of money spare at this time in your life?'

'Daddy'll buy it for me. He gave me his credit card for incidental wedding expenses.'

'Lucky you.'

'Now, how about we make a start on the wedding favours? It's not too late and they're going to take ages.'

'Unlike you, I've had a hectic working day. I have another busy one tomorrow and I need some sleep. I didn't get much last night, worrying about where you were.'

'No need to concern yourself. I was fine.'

'Yes, well I didn't know that, did I? Ian was about to drive round the streets looking for you in case you'd had an accident.'

'Dear man. He worries too much.'

Lori dragged out her carton of materials to make up little boxes of wedding favours for each of the guests. There were packs of chocolate to be put into each one and a flower to stick on the top. She began to try to make up a box and ruined the first one. Matti watched, determined not to be involved, but after a second one was wrecked, she couldn't resist.

'Look, it goes like this.' She made the folds and pressed the pieces together. 'See?'

'I'm hopeless at anything like this. I knew you'd be able to do it. How about you make them up and I'll pop the chocolates inside and stick the flower on?'

'I'll do a few but then I really must go to bed.' They worked silently for an hour until Matti yawned and said she was leaving Lori to it. 'You've seen how they go now, so you can work on.'

'Nah. Think I'll call it a day too. I was pretty late getting to bed last night.'

She was still sleeping when Matti left for work the next morning. She wondered if Lori would ever make it to the bridal shop but she was past caring. The whole wedding was turning into a nightmare and she wanted no part of it, if the truth was told. But, for Ian's sake, she would say no more for now and let things take their course.

'Morning,' Ian said in somewhat despondent tones.

'Morning. You look down. What's wrong?'

'Can we talk later? We've only got

one operation today. The afternoon patient has an infection and so he's been sent home. We haven't offered the cancellation to anyone else. I'm finishing at midday so please can we have lunch?'

'Actually, Sam was hoping to meet you for lunch. He needs to talk to you. We were all going to talk last night but Lori made her claim on you. I'll be delighted to see you later though if you still want to.' He gave a her a look. It wasn't like Matti to be so direct.

'Yes please. What does Sam want?'

'Man talk.' She refused to say more and they set to work.

The operation went well and as she watched Ian's surgical skills once more, she knew that she would find it a great loss to change disciplines, even within the same hospital. Other surgeons certainly had skills, but heart surgery was becoming her passion. The delicacy of the work and the satisfyingly rapid results in patient health were reward enough. Just because she'd saved a little boy did not make her a paediatric specialist.

When Ian had gone for lunch, she went to visit some of their earlier patients in the wards. It was gratifying to see them walking around and getting ready to leave after so few days.

'You know, dear, I never believed I'd be going home only six days after this surgery,' Mrs Howorth said. 'My son is coming to fetch me soon and I'm going to stay with them for a while.'

'That's lovely. You take care though. You've done really well but you must be careful not to catch a cold.'

'Thank you again, dear. And thank that handsome doctor of yours, won't you? You make a lovely couple, and working together too. Must be really nice for you.'

'Oh but we're not a couple. He's getting married soon and unfortunately, not to me.'

'That's silly. You're obviously made for each other. Could see it at once.'

'Some things don't always work out.

Goodbye, Mrs Howorth. Take care.'

Sadly, Matti walked away. Everyone else could see it, but not Ian. She wondered how Sam had got on with his talk. The look on Ian's face gave nothing away when he came back to his office later. Cautiously, Matti smiled at him and raised her eyebrows questioningly. He drew in a deep breath and let rip.

'I suppose this is your doing, is it?' he snapped. 'You put Sam up to this?'

'I'm not sure what you mean exactly.'

'All this stuff about Lori and other men?'

'Well, I did tell him of my concerns.'

'How could you, Matti? I thought you were my friend. My best friend, in fact.'

'Because I'm your friend?' Matti said slowly.

'Some friend. I don't understand what your game was. Why would you spread such evil gossip? Not like you. Not like you at all.'

'I take it you don't believe any of it?'

'Of course not. Lori has explained everything to me. Last night, she told me everything. Including the fact that you are as jealous as hell. No wonder you want to spread gossip about her innocent time spent with others.'

'Her cousin from America, I expect? And she told you about her car being left in Newquay? Her mobile phone getting lost? And as for the rest, let's not even go there.' He stared at her, clearly not knowing what she was talking about.

'You really are something, aren't you? Always playing the innocent. I thought you and Sam might have something going but hearing this, maybe I ought to let him know exactly what you're like.'

'What?' she whispered faintly.

As the room swirled around her, Matti clutched the edge of the desk. This was Ian speaking to her as if she was the worst person on earth. She felt the blood drain from her face and thought she was about to pass out. This could not be happening. This was the very reason she had said nothing but now Ian was accusing her of mischief-making.

'But, Ian . . . I . . . '

'Please spare me any more lies. I don't want to hear them.'

'Right. I'll go then. I assume our chat is off?'

'I'd rather not even see you.'

'And this from the man who said *he* wanted to speak to *me* about some concern he had. You just can't face the truth, can you? Of course I care about you. Sam cares about you. Why else would we be talking about Lori this way?' Ian's face was white. His mouth was clamped into a tense line. He could not speak. 'Do you want to find someone else for the operation tomorrow? You said it was a complex one. Your final one before your . . . your wedding leave.'

'No, you'll have to do it. I can't get anyone else who's trained for this one in time.'

'If there's nothing else, I'll go now then. I'm sure your precious fiancée will appreciate my help at home.'

He looked down at his notes and said nothing. She left the office, still shaking with the shock of his words. He must really love Lori to be taken in by all her lies and for him to think she could make up such things . . . Her phone bleeped. It was a text message from Sam.

Ian took it badly. Avoid him till you've spoken to me. Sam. x

She sent a message back saying it was too late. She added, *Resigning as bridesmaid. Is job offer still open?* He sent another very brief message. *Canteen. Coffee. Now.*

She ordered two coffees and slumped down. A few minutes later Sam rushed in, stethoscope flying out behind him. She pushed a cup towards him.

'So, you and I are both in the dog-house?' she said.

'I totally do *not* understand him. It's as if he's been brainwashed. He didn't want to listen to any of it and made excuses for everything I told him. I don't know what Lori said to him last night but whatever it was, she was very convincing. Tales of cousins from America. Mobile getting lost.'

'That last one was true at least. But it's fine. Daddy will buy her a new one. A much better one than she had before. Look, I'm sorry, but I'm in shock and I feel terrible. I suppose his reaction is understandable. He doesn't want to believe the worst, nor does he want to think he's been fooled.'

'Are you really interested in moving to my department? Was that shock speaking or a serious suggestion?'

'I'll bear it in mind. Ian still wants me to work with him tomorrow. A tricky valve replacement on a fairly young man. Complications ahead, of course. But he says he can't get anyone else with experience in time. I think that he will want to replace me eventually.'

'Maybe Lori will convince him she's a perfect replacement,' he suggested.

Matti snorted. 'If she was in the right mood, of course. She's probably capable of conning him that she's suitable. Look, I've had it for today. I'm going home to see what sort of chaos she's established now. I suppose I feel duty-bound to see it through the next couple of days. Really feel like telling her to go to that place below. I doubt even *Daddy*'s help will get her any better organised. Thank heavens you'll be there to prop me up through it all.' He gave her a comforting hug as she left.

There was no sign of the bride-to-be when Matti returned home. The unmade boxes were still piled on the table as they had been left the previous night and little else had changed. She went and lay on her bed and found tears were rolling down her cheeks. Her worst nightmare was getting worse by the day. She heard Lori come in and someone was with her. She closed her eyes, dreading some new unwanted male in the flat.

'Matti? You home?' she called.

She got up and wiped her face. She

looked terrible. Maybe she could pretend she felt ill. No need to pretend. She certainly felt totally sick.

'Hi. Who's here?'

'God, you look terrible. Hope you're not coming down with anything I might catch before Saturday.'

'I'm sure you are quite safe. So, who's here?'

'I persuaded a couple of friends to come back with me. Help get those dratted boxes done. I wasn't sure you'd be home in time. Time's pressing. Okay, girls. Matti is the expert. She'll show you how it's done and then you can crack on. I'll see you later.'

'Hang on a mo. Where are you going?'

'Have to see if I get the dress fitting done. She was busy this morning so I said I'd drop by this afternoon.'

'And she was all right with that?'

'Wasn't best pleased but for goodness sake, it's my dress and I'm paying her a fortune for it. The least she can do is make sure it fits me. Chiao. See you later.'

'But Lori . . . ' Typically, she had

swept out, not wanting to hear any more. She really was the limit.

'I could murder a cuppa,' one of the girls said.

'Sure. I'll put the kettle on,' Matti muttered helplessly. 'Sorry, I don't know your names.'

'I'm Jean and she's Sally. And you're Matti?'

'That's right. You're friends of Lori's?'

'Not really. We were just chatting in the phone shop. You know, the one at the shopping mall. She was getting in a panic over all she had to do and asked us if we'd come and help her out. Said it was worth a tenner each.'

Matti closed her eyes and shook her head in despair. She wondered what else Lori had promised them. Typical of Lori to persuade two perfect strangers to do a job for her. The sooner the job was done, the sooner she could have the place to herself again. She showed them how to fold the boxes and do the finishing touches. Less than a couple of hours later, they were all finished.

'We'll stack them back in the carton. Thanks,' she added. She wondered when Lori would get back to pay her new friends but there was no sign. How long did a wedding dress fitting take?

'We'll need a lift back into town,' Jean said. 'And the money of course. The bride said you'd sort us out if she wasn't back in time.'

'Oh did she? I'll see if she's left any money in her room.' Naturally, there was nothing. There were several expensive-looking clothing bags lying on the bed. *Daddy*'s credit card had been working overtime by the looks of things but there was no sign of any cash. There was nothing for it but for her to pay up and hope the cash would be returned. Fuming inside, she handed over ten pounds to each of the girls and drove them back into town.

There was still no sign of Lori when she got back. She opened a bottle of wine and decided on a long soak in the bath. Some relaxing bath oil, a scented candle and a glass of wine might help her confused brain to settle down. What a day. What a week. The whole business was a total mess and she was slap-bang in the middle of it. It was beginning to get dark now and still her flatmate hadn't returned. She must have met up with Ian or someone and decided to go on somewhere. Typical.

Deciding she was beginning to wrinkle, she hauled herself out of the water. She dressed in her jeans and a comfy favourite shirt and stared at the beautiful bridesmaid's dress she was supposed to wear in a few days. It was a delicate lilac shade, strapless and with a beaded top that placed it firmly into the higher levels of very expensive. It was the sort of dress she might dream of buying and never be able to afford. She carried it through to Lori's room and hung it on the wardrobe door. She would not be wearing it on Saturday and it was up to the bride to decide if she would find someone else to wear it or return it to the shop.

She noticed the message machine

was flashing. The phone must have rung while she was in the bath.

'Hi,' said Lori's voice. 'It's taken forever at the bridal shop and I've decided I'm going to go home to see my parents for the evening. I'll explain everything tomorrow.' She sounded very subdued for her. Clearly something was wrong. Matti's brain raced. Maybe the dress didn't fit and she was going home to have a tantrum. Who could tell with that girl? Her parents lived in mid-Devon, not too far away. At least Matti would have a peaceful evening on her own. Or so she thought, until the doorbell rang. She brushed back her damp hair with her fingers and straightened her shirt. It was Ian, standing on her doorstep looking pale and very worried.

'Lori's gone to see her parents for the evening,' she said as calmly as she could, her heart racing almost out of control.

'Really? Or are you trying to cover for her?'

'Cover for her? What do you mean? Oh no. Never again. Gone to see her parents. That's what she told me. You can even hear her message on the answering machine.'

'Can I come in?'

'I . . . I'm not sure if it's a good idea.'

'Please. We really need to talk.'

'I feel as if I've heard as much as I want to hear from you today. Which was pretty much what you said to me this afternoon.'

He had the good grace to look ashamed. 'I know I don't deserve it but please, can we talk?'

She held the door open and he came in. His long body slumped down on the creaky old sofa. He looked the picture of misery. She took pity on him and poured him a glass of wine. He took it gratefully.

'So, what did you want to say?' she asked.

'I'm sorry, for starters. Really sorry. I had no right to accuse you of making up all that stuff. I was angry with Sam.

Angry with you. I didn't want to believe any of it and was hitting back. I've been pacing up and down since you left and I saw Sam again. He was quite convincing this time. I just had to see you to clear the air.'

'I see. So do I take it you now believe us? Me and Sam, I mean?'

'Maybe. Some of it. But I'm still not sure why you waited until now to tell me. It's the wedding on Saturday. Why did you wait so long?'

'So long? It's not as if you've been engaged for months. Besides, would you have been more likely to believe me if I'd said something sooner?'

'Probably not. But you painted Lori so very black between you. Is she really as bad as you or Sam, at least, says she is?'

'She really has been going out with other men and certainly has done since you were engaged. I'm not saying she, well, she actually sleeps with them, but one can't help being suspicious when she doesn't come home at night. She said she was having a final fling before married life. What was her phrase? *Settling to the kitchen sink of life.* She says it as if it's a life sentence.' Ian raised his eyebrows but said nothing. She continued. 'And I'm not sure you really know what you're taking on. I can understand that you've been captivated by someone who is undoubtedly gorgeous, full of life and the exact opposite of everything you've been for the last few years. You work so hard and you've done very well for yourself. You're talented and dedicated and it seems to me that you've grabbed at something while it's there and available. As for Lori, I think she is just in love with the idea of a glamorous wedding and a good match.'

'Wow, say it like it is, why don't you? No holding back.'

'Nothing else to lose. I feel as if I've already lost the things that are most important to me in my life. I just want you to be sure you know what you're doing.'

'But I'm not.' Matti stared at him. Was he finally admitting that he had doubts? He lowered his head onto one arm and looked positively exhausted. 'I'm not at all sure about any of it. It's all been much too fast. I'm not even sure it was me who proposed. It just sort of happened and the next thing we were buying a ring.'

Neither of them spoke for a while. Matti re-filled their glasses and they sat staring into space, both busy with their own thoughts. She was suddenly reminded of the day, so long ago, when they had gone to school together to collect their exam results. They had sat side by side staring into space, wondering if they had gained adequate grades to follow their chosen professions. He was a year ahead but they both knew they needed particular grades for the exams they had done. They had gripped each other's hands, asking each other every few seconds . . . *what if?* She smiled at him and touched his hand.

'Remember when we . . . '

'We were waiting for our exam results? Funny, I was just thinking about that too. We go back a long way, don't we? Why haven't you ever found anyone?'

'I think maybe I did once, but he didn't feel the same way about me,' she replied enigmatically.

'I didn't know that. Someone at college?' She gave a noncommittal shrug. He didn't even guess she meant him. 'I know this has all been very difficult for you and you must have found it awful to have to tell me about the real Lori. But you and I have known each other far too long to have this . . . this cloud between us. Besides, we have to work together.'

'I'm thinking of taking up Sam's offer of a new place in his department.'

'But you can't.' His face looked slightly panic-stricken. 'You really can't. You'd be wasted there. You know as much as any of the registrars I work with. I rely on you one hundred percent. For heaven's sake, Matti, we've been friends forever.' He reached for her hand and took it gently. He kissed her fingertips and she felt as if she were suddenly floating on air. Her emotions had run through every possible phase today and she felt drained. He stood up and held out his hand to her. He put his arms round her and pulled her close. She reached for his beautiful mouth and pressed her own lips to his. He kissed her back and held her. He released her slightly and stroked her loose hair.

'You're beautiful, Matti. I wish I'd seen just how lovely, much sooner. I feel so bad about you.'

'You never even guessed when we went to that end-of-year ball together?'

'I . . . I suspect I got rather drunk then. The relief of having got through some tough exams. But I do remember you looked wonderful and we danced for most of the evening. It was the champagne buffet that was my downfall. Afterwards, I was so ashamed of the way I treated you that I tried to put it all behind me.'

'You did become rather unwell. I

never really minded about that, but it was the way you seemed to ignore me for days afterwards. Well, that was the difficult bit. I'd spent a fortune on the dress as well. A fortune in my terms, not Lori's of course.'

'What do you mean?'

'Lori has very expensive tastes. She has *Daddy* twisted round her little finger and I know that she sees a top surgeon as a reasonable replacement for *Daddy*'s bankroll. Oh lord, I'm sorry. I'm getting so horribly bitchy.'

'Maybe I needed to know. She does always look great. I never really gave much consideration to how she could afford so many clothes. Oh Matti, I'm sorry.'

'Stop apologising.'

'I've been such a fool and an idiot, but I'm afraid it's too late now. I have to marry her. She's . . . no.'

'She's what?'

'Nothing. I gave her my promise and everything's arranged. I have to stick by it. It's simply too late to cancel the wedding now. I'd like to postpone it till

you're better but I doubt she'd agree.'
He put his arm round her shoulder and
she snuggled against him. He kissed her
again, clinging to her for comfort. 'Oh
heavens, I'm sorry, I really shouldn't
have done that. I'm not being fair to
you.'

'No you're not being fair at all. But
it's time I said it. I love you, Ian. I have
always loved you. I waited for you to say
something first, stupid woman that I
am. I never dared risk saying it first in
case you didn't feel the same. And now
I suspect I've made even more of a fool
of myself. You'd better go before I do
anything even more ridiculous. There's
no point me trying to make you be
unfaithful. I'd hate you to compare me
to her.'

'But I never would.'

'If you're not sure about her, then why
are you going ahead with this wedding?'

'I have to.'

'But you don't, Ian. It isn't too late.
Yes, it will be difficult to cancel it, but
surely a few complications are better

than a divorce in a year or two, or even a lifetime of unhappiness.'

'I have to marry her. Subject closed.'

'But you seem so far apart from everything she stands for. There are so many things you don't share. Music. Clubs. And has she decided to overhaul your house? Make changes everywhere?'

'We haven't really discussed it much. I guess we shall do all that sort of thing once we're both living there.'

'Oh Ian. I can't believe you're . . . Oh I don't know. For such an intelligent, talented man, you're just so naïve.' She shook her head in helpless frustration. 'I really hope it works out for you and that you're not building up a store of unhappiness. I know I have no right to interfere but you don't even realise half the truth. Lori's not the easiest person to live with. She's got little or no sense of responsibility and relies on her parents to bail her out whenever the going gets tough. She leaves everything lying around for me to put away. Never thinks of buying any groceries or cleaning materials. Not that she'd know what to do with them if she did. Usually a month behind with the rent, and that after only three months living here. Okay, I'll shut up now. I've said more than enough. But believe me, you are my only concern.'

'I'm so sorry, Matti. I do have deep feelings for you. As you say, and we both realise, it's all too late. Maybe we should both have spoken out earlier. It was me that you thought was the some-one special at college, wasn't it?' She nodded. He reached for her once more and tried to give her a gentle, comfort-ing hug. He felt her tension and drew away. He kissed her cheek and regret-fully, left the flat.

She touched the place on her cheek that he had kissed and felt as if her whole world was in tatters. She poured the last of the wine into her glass and drained it. She drew in her breath, gritted her teeth and vowed she had cried her last over Ian Faulkner. She hoped she could keep her vow.

6

Perhaps it was the wine or plain emotional exhaustion, but Matti slept surprisingly well that night and woke refreshed. It was Thursday and Ian's last day at work before the wedding. She arrived early and went to check on the theatre. Unusually, Ian had not put in appearance by eight o'clock. The more complex operations were usually well underway by this time. She went into the office and glanced at the patient file and careful notes Ian had made in his awful green ink. The phone rang. It was the ward sister, asking for instructions regarding the patient.

'Mr Faulkner is not available at the moment,' she said, 'so I suggest you delay the pre-med. I'll call you as soon as I know more.' She put the phone down and then dialled Ian's mobile. It was switched off. She began to panic slightly.

Where was he? He never switched his mobile off and was always the most reliable of people. She dialled Sam's number in case he had any news, but he had heard nothing. She was at a loss. Ian would never let anyone down unless it was a dire emergency. She was on the verge of checking the police in case there had been an accident when he finally arrived. His face was grey and dark lines under his eyes suggested a lack of sleep.

'Sorry,' he muttered. 'I've asked Craig Jenkins to scrub in with us today. I'm not feeling too good but I can't let our patient down. He really can't afford to wait any longer for his op and he's relying on me.'

'You sure you're okay to do this? You look dreadful.'

'Didn't sleep much. You know. Stuff going round and round in my brain. I was walking round the streets at three o'clock. I was trying to decide what to do for the best.'

'Only you can decide. You know my thoughts.'

'I can't let Lori down and all the guests who are coming. Presents and everything. All the arrangements. Oh it's all just too much to change things at this stage.'

'You are talking about the rest of your life. Still, there's always divorce if you really don't make a go of it. Expensive business but hey, what's all that against a few altered plans and someone possibly being hurt? Sorry. That was nasty of me. I guess my emotions are pretty wrung out too.' He looked completely drained and was about to embark on a life-threatening, life-saving operation. 'So, is Craig going to lead or are you?'

'I think it has to be Craig's call. I know this particular case well but I'm sure he's done this op many times before.'

Matti felt somewhat nervous. It was so out of character for Ian to be in this state, and Craig was a much older man with a reputation for being impatient with his theatre staff. She just hoped she wouldn't be the one to let Ian down.

'Shall I call the ward then? They rang and I told them to hang back with the final stages of the pre-med for a while.'

'Thanks. Yes. I'll get to theatre and prime Craig. You come down when you're ready.'

The operation lasted for a very long time, despite having two surgeons and full theatre staff in attendance. There were a number of crises and at one point, they thought they were losing their patient. But their skills paid off and he was revived. It was almost two o'clock before they were finished. Craig had proved himself very capable of leading the op and Ian had supported perfectly.

'Thanks, everyone. Good job,' he called out as he was leaving. 'Craig, thanks. I owe you. I'm sorry to lay this on you at short notice.'

'No problem. But you should get yourself checked over. You look terrible. More than wedding nerves, I'd say. Is there anything I can help with?'

'Not at all thanks. Just a minor crisis, and I hardly slept the last couple of nights. Maybe I should have given myself a longer break before the big day. There seems to be a load of stuff still to be done. I never realised a relatively simple ceremony would involve so much hassle and rushing around. Anyway, that's me done now for a couple of weeks.' He wrote up his notes and cleared his desk. He intended to call in the next day to check on his patient even though he knew that the other teams would make sure all was well. He sat, head in hands, wondering what he should do next. He knew that he really needed to see Lori and talk things through but he felt that he couldn't face it. What did that tell him about their relationship?

Matti came into the office. 'You all right?' she asked, putting a cup of coffee on the desk.

'Thanks. No, not really. But I still don't know what to do for the best.'

'Go home and get some sleep. You

look exhausted, and you can't make any rational decisions until you've had some proper rest.'

'I should see Lori though. There are things we need to say to each other. Will she be back from her parents?'

'How should I know? Ring her and see. But please, get some rest first. Take a pill if you need to, but try and get rid of that awful grey look you have about you.'

'Are you going back to the flat? You could ring me if she's there.'

'You know, I don't think I am. I'm going down to the beach to walk a bit and I plan to get some good, fresh air. It's a nice afternoon and it will do me far more good than stewing in the flat. I'm sorry but I also need a complete break from wedding preparations, and especially a break from Lori. I'll see you later.' She left him still sitting slumped in his chair. She had the next day off, mainly to help Lori with final preparations, but just at this moment she could hardly bear to look at her flatmate. On her way down to the hospital car park, her phone rang. It was Lori.

'Matti? Where are you? I really need to see you. Can you come home or should I come and meet you somewhere?'

'I'm just going out. Is it urgent?'

'Really urgent. Please, come home if you can.'

'All right. On my way.' She drove back, wondering if there really was something wrong or whether it was just another Lori ploy to get her to do something.

'I've made some tea. And there's a chocolate muffin for you. Thought you might need a chocolate fix.'

Matti raised her eyebrows. It was unusual for her to be so thoughtful. 'Thanks. I missed lunch so that's very welcome. What's up?'

'You hung your bridesmaid dress in my room. I wondered why?'

'I was so mad at you. You've taken me for granted just one too many times. I decided I'm not going to be your bridesmaid after all. You might like to take the dress back to the shop or find someone else to wear it. Is that all you wanted me for?'

'No. But it was the last straw.' Her eyes filled with tears. 'The dress fitting last night. Oh Matti, it's awful. I must have put on weight and I look dreadful in it. Bulges here and there that were never there when I tried it on before. The stupid woman says she can't do anything about it. It's impossible to let it out without making marks. I said I'd have another dress and picked one out. She said I'd still have to pay for the first one as well in case she couldn't re-sell it. I don't see why not, but there you go. So, I picked this other one . . . a really gorgeous one, and I think I liked it even better than the first one. Cost a fortune of course, but I used Daddy's card and well, it was maxed out. When I rang my parents, they said I'd have to pay my own bills from now on. Even when I explained everything, they said no. That's why I went home, to try to persuade them, but they were still adamant . . . they won't pay for another dress.'

'So pay for it yourself, if you really want to change it at this late stage.'

'I can't. I'm broke. Can you lend me some money? I'd ask Ian but it seems unfair to ask him to pay for my actual wedding dress.'

'No way can I lend you that sort of money. Just settle for the dress you've got and hold your stomach in. You can't have put that much weight on in five weeks.'

Lori looked away and moaned on. 'I can't believe my parents want to ruin the biggest day of my life.'

'Oh for goodness sake. Stop being a drama queen. The dress you picked is perfectly nice as it is. Stunning, in fact. You're dreaming if you think it's awful.'

'But everyone will be looking at me. All the photographs, everything. You're a perfect shape and your dress fits you like a glove. You'll end up stealing the whole show.'

'Grow up, Lori. Just go to the bridal shop again and say you'll settle for the dress you chose. Wear a girdle or something if it's that bad. You don't have a choice. And if you're short of cash, take back some of those expensive goodies lying on your bed. And by the way, you still owe me twenty quid for those two women you picked up to make your wedding things. I had to pay them myself and I need it back.'

'Course you'll get it back. I don't know what's come over you. Why are you being so nasty to me? But you are still going to be my bridesmaid, aren't you? I'll never find anyone else at this late stage.'

'I suppose you won't. I'll think about it but I don't hold out any hopes. Now, I'm going out. I've got a splitting headache and I need some air. Go and sort out your dress before it's too late.' Lori drew breath to speak. 'No,' Matti snapped. 'I will not come with you. Do something for yourself for once.' Lori picked up her handbag and keys and tried once more to persuade Matti to go with her, but she remained adamant. 'No. Go and sort yourself out.'

'Why are you being so nasty to me? I'd like the old Matti back. The one who always helps me out.'

'Saint Matti the martyr is dead. This is the new me.'

She watched as the girl slammed the door and drove off. She turned back into the flat and heard the phone ringing. It was Ian.

'Why aren't you asleep?' she asked him.

'I couldn't rest. I need to speak to Lori.'

'She's just gone out. Wedding dress crisis. She says it doesn't fit her anymore. I told her not to be so stupid. She can't have put on weight in a few weeks.'

'She probably has. Matti, she's pregnant. That's why I have to marry her.'

'What?' Matti almost screamed.

'She's pregnant.'

'But she can't be. I mean, how do you know?'

'She's done a test. Says it was positive.'

'But she's not shown any symptoms. No morning sickness or anything.'

'Not everyone does have morning sickness. You know that.'

'But are you sure it's yours? I mean, in light of everything we know about her?'

'Matti, you're clutching at straws. Lori assures me she's pregnant with my child. Obviously, it's early days yet. But I can only believe what she says.'

'You're probably the only person who does,' she said bitterly. 'Well, I suspect that making beds and lying in them springs to mind. I can't talk any more. I expect Lori will be back later. Sorry but I have to go out now.' She slammed the phone down. Her emotions were shattered and she felt more angry than she had ever felt in her life before. Lori pregnant? She couldn't bear to be in the flat seeing all of Lori's things littering the place. Wedding favours. Piles of presents and wedding paper filling the waste bin. Lori had torn every parcel open the minute it had arrived. She'd bitten off Matti's head when she had suggested Ian might like to share in opening their presents.

'Rubbish,' she snapped. 'Why would he be interested? Oh heavens, just look at this hideous jug and glasses set. Who on earth would use that?'

'Someone chose it for you.'

'My ancient aunt who never had any taste at all. Hope Ian's got plenty of cupboard space.'

Matti closed her eyes at the memory. She picked up her keys and handbag and slammed the door as she left.

Furiously, she drove away from the flat with no definite destination in mind. She just needed to get away and think. Lori's wedding dress crisis was a matter of vanity and little more. The pregnancy was something entirely different. No wonder her wedding dress didn't fit properly. But when had it happened? And was Ian really the father? Was this the whole reason for the rather hastily arranged marriage? How could she? Trapping someone into marriage like that was despicable. Especially when it was Ian.

Matti drove down to a parking spot near the beach. It was one of her favourite places and somewhere she often came to relax. Pity she hadn't put her trainers in the car or she could have gone for a run along the cliff top. Her anger might have dissipated a little with an energetic run. The views from there were spectacular and not too many people went along that way, more than a few yards from the car park. Instead, she went down on the beach and took off her shoes and went into the edge of the sea and paddled along the water's edge. Little waves broke over her feet and she felt the water relaxing her. It was warm, almost warm enough to swim. But she rarely swam these days. A few years ago, in the days before university, great crowds of them used to meet at the beach and swim and surf and have late-night beach parties.

Where had those days gone? Ian was always there and they'd more often than not been together. Never exactly a couple, but always something special and understood between them, or so she had thought. Being a year older than her had meant nothing.

She sat on a rock, dreaming of the past for half an hour. But that was the past, and over and done with. She went back up towards the car park.

She saw two teenagers with a young dog also walking up from the beach. They were holding hands and stopped to kiss. Matti smiled. They were wrapped in their own little world and wandered back up the road, taking no notice of anyone or anything else. The dog suddenly spotted another dog and wrenched the lead out of their hands. They shrieked after it to come back but it was having a high old time and totally ignored their cries. A bus approached and the dog bounded into the road again. Matti called to the dog and it stopped and turned. The bus stopped and she ran forward to try and catch the dog. As she did so, another car came rushing along the road from the opposite direction, loud music beating out and its young driver travelling much too fast. The dog ran in front of her, tripping her over as the car smashed straight into her, knocking her flat over the bonnet. In slow motion, she rolled off and into the road.

'Idiot woman,' the young driver yelled. 'What the heck are you playing at?' one of the others in the car leaned out of the window and screamed.

'She's hurt pretty badly. You'd better drive off fast. Back up and turn round. You're not even supposed to be out in your brother's car. He'll kill you when he finds out,' one of the boy's passengers was screaming.

Everyone was shouting at everyone else. There was no way the car could drive away with the crowd that was gathering. The passengers had got off the bus and several people were already using their mobiles to call an ambulance.

Matti lay still, vaguely hearing all the noise and shouting but totally immobile and unaware of what was really happening. Subconsciously, she was desperately trying to draw air into her lungs but it felt as if an elephant was sitting on top of her. The impact had winded her completely. She knew that moving any part of her might cause damage so she lay still, willing herself not to stir a muscle, even if she could. Vague areas of pain were beginning to filter into her consciousness. Her arm and one shoulder were beginning to send sharp stabs through her. Could she sense a trickle of blood on her forehead? Her eyes were shut tight and she was as white as the proverbial sheet.

After what seemed an age of shouting and noise, the ambulance's siren sounded. At the same time, a police car arrived. The paramedics insisted on everyone moving away. She felt as if she were watching some film and even with her eyes closed, she knew she could see what was happening. It was all too weird.

'Give us some space and let's see what we can do to help this poor lady. Anyone know who she is?' one of the paramedics asked the group gathered round.

'Nah. She was just walking along towards the car park. The dog ran out and she tried to catch it.'

'Ran straight in front of me, she did. Couldn't do nuffink to save her,' the driver of the car said quickly. 'They'll all say the same, won't you, lads? She just came out of nowhere.' He was shaking and had already lit a cigarette in trembling fingers. His passengers were gathered behind him, looking terrified. They all looked less than fifteen years old.

'Can I see your licence please,' the policeman said to him.

'Bit awkward like. I came out in a hurry and didn't pick it up.'

'I see. And your insurance certificate the same, I suppose? Don't you know you're supposed to carry your documents at all times?'

'Yer, well I forgot, din' I? Anyroad, I thought you could always take them into the station later on.'

'Oh yes, you'll certainly need to do that. I take it this is your vehicle?'

'It's partly mine. Me and me brother share it.'

'And you're driving it with his permission?'

'Don't need it if we both own it, do we?'

'And how old are you, exactly?'

'Old enough. You can't go picking on me just because I look young.'

'I haven't finished with you yet. Just stay where you are,' the officer said fiercely.

The two policemen moved on to take statements from the witnesses and the other young occupants of the car. This conversation was going on in the background while the paramedics were working on Matti. They had fixed a neck collar on her and were busily engaged in sliding a back board under her to lift her into the ambulance.

Despite her eyes still being firmly closed, she later told them that she remembered hearing the conversation between the policeman and the young driver.

'Can you hear me, love?' someone was shouting in her ear.

'Yes,' she was saying, or thought she was saying.

'Haven't we seen her somewhere?' one of them said. 'I've got a feeling she works at the hospital. I have visions of seeing her in blue scrubs.'

'She's got car keys clutched in her hand. Maybe we can try pressing the remote unlock and locate her car. There might be some identification in it. Officer, can you come over here a minute?'

The paramedic and policeman conferred and indeed found her car. Her handbag was under the seat and her documents and hospital identity card were all there.

'Matti Harper. She's a theatre sister in the cardiac department.'

'Matti? Matti, can you hear me? You've had an accident and we're taking you to hospital now.'

She whispered something and finally risked opening her eyes. It was all very bright and the light hurt her eyes. She couldn't move anything and lay on the stretcher fearing the worst. Her arms and legs were completely still and try as she might, nothing would move. She whimpered out loud. She was totally paralysed and totally terrified. What would she do? How could she live if she couldn't move?

'It's all right, love. We'll give you something for the pain.'

Her mouth felt full of something that was preventing her from speaking and she tried to shake her head to say she wasn't in pain.

'She's in distress. Let's get her to hospital asap. Her vital signs are actually okay but there's something going on we can't see. Okay, stand back please.' They wheeled the trolley into the ambulance and she was aware of the doors closing and engine revving. She heard the siren start up and worried that she was seriously hurt if they needed to rush her to the hospital with such urgency. It was a terrifying noise.

Gradually, people drifted away. The police decided they needed to escort the teenaged car-driver back to his home to find out the real truth about his age and if anything at all he had said was true. It was a subdued group by this time and the loud music had been turned off.

'Lock her car, Charlie. We'll send someone back for it and take it back to the yard till she's ready to use it again.'

The dog had been recaptured and soon the beach was returned to normal. Matti's little blue car sat on its own in the car park until it could be retrieved.

7

By the time they had driven back to
A&E, Matti's eyes were fully open and
she was beginning to recover a little.
Her middle felt sore and she realised
she'd been completely winded. The
oxygen mask over her mouth prevented
proper speech but at least she was
aware of what was going on and
beginning to be able to communicate
again. She had also realised that she
wasn't after all totally paralysed. She
had been wrapped very tightly in a
blanket, to stop her moving and damag-
ing anything while they lifted her. She
giggled slightly hysterically at the realisa-
tion and wondered if she'd ever dare
confess her thoughts to anyone. Ian
would laugh about it when she told
him. Ian. With a new start of recogni-
tion she remembered the dratted wedding.
It seemed that fate had taken a hand

and she would not have to be a brides-maid after all. She might even escape attending the whole thing.

'Okay, on my count. Everyone got a piece? One, two, three.' She was lifted onto the bed and unwrapped from her blanket.

'Hi, Matti. I'm Doctor Flemming. Can you tell me where it hurts?'

'Round the middle. My arm's sore and well, everywhere feels sort of battered, really. My mouth is sore and my head hurts. Sorry, I sound a wreck. I'm not used to being on this side of the counter.'

'Yes, I gather you work here. Is there anyone you'd like me to call for you?'

'Ian. Mr Faulkner please. His number's on my mobile.'

'Your mobile's a bit the worse for wear, I'm afraid. But Ian's on our list anyway. Right, let's get X-rays of her arm, and as she was out for a long time, better organise a head scan. We'll do an ultra-sound over the midriff area just to make sure there's nothing nasty going on there.' The doctor called for the usual screening tests and asked if she needed any more pain relief. She refused, saying everything was just a dull ache and she felt muzzy enough without anything else. For the next hour, she seemed to be taken from one machine to the next with people prodding and moving her, albeit gently enough. She had bitten her tongue during the impact and her mouth was better once she had rinsed out the blood.

At last Ian was standing beside her. He took her hand and kissed her fingertips.

'Sorry to bother you. You're probably desperately busy,' she said softly.

'Don't be silly. I couldn't get here fast enough when they called me. Are you sure they're looking after you properly? Doing all the tests and everything? I'll have a word with the consultant in a minute when I've made sure you're all right. Is there anything I can get for you? Do you want me to call your parents?'

'No of course not. They're on holiday

in Spain and I don't want them flying back to fuss over me.'

'Okay then. Don't go away. I'm going to speak to Doctor Flemming. He's a good bloke so I'm sure he'll do all that's necessary.'

'I'm hardly likely to go anywhere, am I? Trapped in this bed. I never realised what it feels like to be stuck in one of these beds and not allowed to move. I shall view our patients with a lot more sympathy in future.'

'I've no doubt you'll be a terrible patient.' He went away and she gazed at his comforting presence as he spoke to the doctor. He picked up her notes and read through them, nodding as he saw everything. She wanted to call out, *I understand medical matters too, you know. Don't cut me out of it. It's my body we're discussing here.* She challenged him when he came back.

'So, what was all the nodding and note-reading about? You might as well tell me everything.'

'You probably have a badly sprained

wrist. They'll know more later. Bruising round the rib cage but nothing broken. Lucky you. Mind you, you have a decent-sized cut over one eye. Don't worry, it can be repaired without spoiling your beauty. There's a massive bruise on your shoulder and you'll be sporting a large strapping on your wrist for the foreseeable future.'

'And that's it? I'm not paralysed forever more?'

'Why did you think that?'

'Tight blanket wrapping in the ambulance. When I found that I couldn't move my arms or legs, I did wonder.' She looked at him as his eyes began to crinkle at the corners. His mouth twitched and he finally gave in and laughed. She tried to look cross but she too began to laugh. 'It wasn't funny at the time. I had no idea what had hit me. All the air was knocked out of me for a while and I could scarcely draw breath without it hurting.'

'My poor darling. I was terrified when I got the call. I was having my hair cut and the poor barber wondered what had hit him. I expect I'm all lopsided.'

'You look great to me,' Matti whispered. 'Thank you for coming. I didn't know who else to ask.'

'Of course you would ask for them to call me.'

'Good job it wasn't next week or you'd be off in sunnier climes.'

He gave a start. 'I suppose I'd better call Lori. She'll be wondering what's happened to you.'

'I doubt she'll have noticed I'm not there. She's having a wedding dress crisis. You nearly got saddled with the bill for another dress, but hopefully I persuaded her there's nothing wrong with it.'

'You're beginning to sound more normal again. I can't tell you how scared I was. Oh my darling Matti. When I thought you might be . . . I couldn't bear it if you weren't in my life.'

He sat beside her bed, holding her good hand. When they were satisfied that all the tests were normal, she was allowed to sit in a wheelchair and go to the plaster room for her wrist to be strapped.

'But I thought it wasn't broken?'

'It isn't, but you have a bad sprain and it needs to be firmly strapped to prevent any movement. They'll be looking at it again tomorrow. And I suspect the shoulder is going to need some support too. I'll give Lori a call while that's happening. She needs to know what's going on.' Ian walked outside, knowing at last what he wanted to do. He would have to see Lori later, when they could talk in private. He hoped she would co-operate with his suggestions.

An hour later, Matti was back in the A&E department. Her arm was strapped up and she had a sling to support it. Her forehead was stitched and she was beginning to ache all over. Ian came to sit beside her.

'Lori's on her way in. Insisted on coming. The doctor says you can go home this evening but you must agree to going straight to bed and resting. I said I would come and stay at your flat to make sure all was well with you. Hope that's all right with you?'

'That sounds great.'

The door opened and Lori burst in. She gave a scream when she saw Matti. 'Oh my god! What have you done? How can you possibly be a bridesmaid looking like that? It will ruin all the photographs. Oh Matti, how could you do this to me?'

'Thanks for the sympathy. Of course I deliberately set out to be run down. I am actually going to be fine, thanks for asking.'

'Oh I'm sorry. It was the shock of seeing you all battered and bruised.'

'Well, at least I wouldn't have stolen the limelight. You were worried at one point that I might look slimmer than you. I take it you've sorted your dress?'

'I think so. She's agreed to make some alterations and I guess it will look all right. I'm wondering though if I shouldn't see if I can find someone else to take over your bridesmaid duties? You probably won't be feeling up to it anyway. There's a nurse I've worked with on one of the wards who's about your size and shape.'

'Lori,' Ian said in the coldest voice either girl had ever heard from him. 'Lori, why don't you give just a little thought to Matti for once? Just stop trying to turn everything round to how it might affect you. For once, let someone else's needs be centre stage. She's been badly injured and all you can think about it is whether she will ruin your wedding pictures. Now, I'm driving Matti back to the flat in a little while and I shall stay there and make sure she is properly looked after.'

'I can look after her. After all, I am a nurse, you know.'

'I certainly wouldn't have known it from your recent behaviour.'

Lori's eyes filled with tears. She spoke in a little girlish, wailing voice. 'I've been under such stress lately. I don't know how you can be so nasty to me. You know why I'm so stressed. Ian, my darling, please don't look at me that way. This is such a big event in our lives and it's only two days away ... less, really. I can understand that you must be as stressed as I am. I completely forgive you for sounding so unkind to me.'

Ian clamped his mouth shut in a straight line. This was neither the time nor place and if he said anything at all, it would turn into a full-blown tirade. He tucked Matti's blanket round her and wheeled her towards the door. He signed the various papers necessary for her discharge, as it was her right wrist that was damaged and she was incapable of doing it for herself. Lori trailed behind them.

'Right, I'm going to fetch my car. Stay here with Matti until I get back,' he instructed his fiancée.

Both girls were wrapped in their own thoughts. For the first time in ages, Matti was beginning to have hopes.

Ian's reaction to her accident showed her that he really did care, and his shortness with Lori made her think that he now realised what she was really like. Even she had been shocked by the girl's reaction to the accident. No concern for Matti, just concerned that the photographs would be spoilt at the wedding . . . if there was still going to be one.

'It's a nice car, Ian's, isn't it?' Lori said conversationally. 'Bet it's great to drive. I'm looking forward to racing round the roads in France. I can't wait for a turn behind the wheel. We're driving all the way down to the Med, you know.'

'Really,' Matti replied. Ian stopped his car beside her.

'I'm not going to belt you in as it may be painful for you. I'll drive very carefully, don't worry.'

'What about me?' Lori said.

'What about you? Haven't you got your car?'

'Oh, yes of course. I forgot. I thought you might like me to come with you.'

'No point. We'd only have to recover your car later.' They drove back at a very modest speed and Ian took great care not to swing the car round corners or cause any discomfort to his passenger. 'Thank goodness you live on the ground floor. I don't fancy carrying you up a flight of stairs. I would, of course, but this is preferable. You all right? You're very quiet.'

'I'm okay. Just beginning to feel the shock setting in I guess.'

'We'll soon have you in bed and resting. Have you got any food in? I bet you haven't eaten all day.'

'You're right. We sort of missed out on lunch and now it's late for supper as well. I think there may be some eggs. We could have an omelette or something. Actually, should I be eating anything, anyway?'

'Something light will be fine.'

'What it is to have my own personal doctor on hand.'

'Yes, well my being here was the only reason they let you out. Normally, you'd have been kept in overnight. I thought you'd prefer it.'

'Thanks again. I'm glad to be home. But I don't want to be in bed. I'll lie on the sofa'

He was busying himself in the kitchen, looking for ingredients for supper, when Lori arrived back.

'Hi both. Oh goody, are you making supper? I'm starving. It's been quite a day. I'll just go and freshen up and see if I can find some wine. Nice surprise to have you staying here, darling.' She put her arms round Ian's middle but he did not respond. She gave a shrug and went into her room.

A few minutes later, Ian came in with Matti's supper laid on a tray. He'd found some salad and set it alongside a delicious-looking omelette.

'Wow, that looks amazing.'

'Good. Eat it while it's hot. Can you manage with one hand? I cut up the salad small so you can just use a fork. Back in a mo. Mine should be almost ready now.'

He came back with a second tray and sat beside Matti on the creaky sofa. Lori came in.

'Where's mine?'

'I thought you'd probably manage to make your own. Wasn't sure how long you'd be. There are more eggs in the fridge.'

'Thanks a bunch. Is there something wrong? Have I offended you in some way?'

'I'll make a list when I've finished eating,' Ian snapped. She glared at him and then turned to Matti.

'What have you been saying? Have you been trying to poison him against me? You still want him for yourself, don't you? Well tough. He's got to marry me.' She turned to Ian. 'She hates me because you love me and not her.'

'Your reaction to Matti's accident was enough to show me what you're really like, if I hadn't already guessed. You're a spoilt, selfish child. I admit, I'd like to call the whole thing off. But, under the circumstances, I have to stand by you.'

'You love me, Ian. I love you. You're just over-reacting after this damned accident. We're going to have the most beautiful wedding ever. Dozens of people are coming. We've had gorgeous presents from everyone. The flowers, the meal, everything. I took such care choosing them all.'

'It's just a day, Lori. One day in our lives. Why is it such a big deal?'

'What you're really saying is that you'd rather it was Matti you were marrying.'

'Maybe. But you've somehow allowed yourself to become pregnant, despite claiming you couldn't possibly be.'

'Are you quite sure it's Ian's baby?' Matti asked.

But Lori wasn't listening. She was slumping down in the armchair and beginning to sob loudly. 'You are being horrid to me. Both of you. I'm pregnant. I'm in an emotional state. I deserve to be loved. To be looked after. My parents would have killed me if they knew about the baby and I wasn't married.'

Matti went back to eating her meal. Ian sat in grim silence. At last Lori spoke between her slightly hysterical sobs. 'How can you be so cold and heartless? I really thought you loved me, Ian Faulkner.' She almost snarled, 'I really thought I'd found my dream man.'

Matti turned to look at Ian. His face was white and drawn. He was clearly in shock. He pushed his tray to one side and got up. He went outside the flat and stood breathing in the night air. He put his head in his hands and cursed himself roundly for being so stupid. He saw car headlights coming into the flat's communal car park. It was Sam. He felt a surge of relief with the arrival of someone he could actually talk to.

'Ian? I just heard the news. How's Matti? Is she all right?' he asked.

'Sort of. Nothing too serious. I suppose it's all round the hospital?' Sam nodded. 'Oh Sam, how could I have been such a total idiot?'

'Natural talent, old mate. So what's

the latest? Why are you a total idiot on this occasion?'

'I've realised I don't love Lori. I love Matti. I have loved her all the time, but I just didn't realise it till I thought she was . . . that I thought I was going to lose her. When I saw her lying there all battered and bruised, I realised my world would come to an end if I lost her.'

'About time you realised it.'

'How did you know?'

'Obvious when you think about it. You're on exactly the same wavelength. She's gorgeous and she adores you.'

'Took me too long to realise it. But there's nothing I can do about it now.'

'You're not married yet.'

'It's too late. Believe me.'

'Why?'

'It's Lori. She's pregnant.'

'Crikey. That's a shock. I'd have thought you'd be more careful than that. Is it what you want?'

'Not in the least. But I can't let her down now, can I?'

'What a mess. Let's go inside. I'd like to make sure you're doing everything for Matti. Medically, I mean.'

Sam put his hand companionably on Ian's shoulder and they went back inside. Lori had gone into her room, leaving Matti lying on the sofa, her eyes closed.

'Matti, how are you doing?' Sam said, leaning over to kiss her cheek.

'How nice to see you, Sam. Maybe you can instill a little sanity in this place. Evidently Lori's life is now officially over as her parents are probably going to kill her. You know something? I'm totally exhausted by it all. I just don't know what to believe any more. She insists this is Ian's baby but I truly doubt it.' She stared at Ian and he shook his head.

'You surely don't have any doubts?' Sam asked. 'Not if you're marrying the girl?'

'I don't know what to believe. If everything you two say is true.'

'What a mess. What do you say, Sam? Shall you and I just get plastered together?' Matti suggested.

'I think maybe you should go to bed. But I'll certainly take up your offer another day. You've had pain relief so it wouldn't be the best to have anything alcoholic. Shall we help you to bed? Acting together, you'll have two chaper-ones, even if we are both males. Tomorrow, we'll see if there's anything we can salvage from this unhappy situation.'

8

Matti had a series of weird dreams, partly because of the huge flurry of emotions and the medication she had been given. Ian heard Matti stumbling around before seven o'clock the next morning. He made some tea and took it to her room.

'Hey you, what are you doing out of bed? I was going to bring you some breakfast in a minute.'

'I needed to get up. There's going to be masses to do and I just couldn't stay still any longer. Did you sleep at all? You don't look as if you did.'

'Not much. Your sofa is little more than an instrument of torture. How about you?'

'Surprisingly well. Something to do with all the painkillers, no doubt. But I'm not in any real pain at all. Expect I look pretty terrible.'

'You need to rest for a while longer. But remember you have to go to the hospital this morning to have a check-up.'

'Oh really? Why?'

'They needed to check on your wrist.'

'If you say so. What's been going on here?'

'Lori went rushing off to see her parents, I gather. I asked her last night if we could postpone the wedding for a while but she went berserk. Said everyone would already be on their way. Said that even if I didn't love her anymore, we had to go ahead with everything for the baby's sake. I pointed out that people were broader-minded these days and offered to support her at all times.'

'But she wasn't having any of it?'

'Course not. She wants her dream wedding and I'm part of it.'

'So why has she gone home?'

'To drag her parents back to sort me out, I don't doubt. Now drink your tea and I'll make some toast. Then I'll help you get ready. Sam's coming round later and we're taking you to the clinic for your check-up.'

It was nice to be looked after and Matti relaxed. At least she would be spared her duties at the wedding tomorrow. Somehow, knowing Ian loved her seemed to help even if it was now futile and all too late. Perhaps she and Sam might have some sort of future together? She shook her head at the thought. Obviously, the effects of the medication were still in her system. An hour later, they were sitting in the out-patients clinic. Ian went off to look at his patient of yesterday and Sam sat with her.

'Terrible places, these hospitals, aren't they?' he remarked.

'Certainly are. Never go near them myself,' Matti giggled. 'Ouch, that hurts.'

'Only when you laugh, I assume.'

'Matti Harper? This way please.' The nurse ushered her through to the consulting room. Sam assisted her but left her to go in on her own.

'The doctor will be with you in a minute. We're short-staffed today. One of our nurses is getting married tomorrow and we still haven't managed to find a replacement.'

Matti sat alone in the curtained cubicle. The nurse in question must be Lori. She heard the nurse who had shown her through chatting to someone else in the next cubicle. She could tell from the sounds that they were changing the sheets.

'Looks like it's all go ahead for Lori after all.'

'Thought it was all fixed anyway.'

'Well, she told me a few weeks back that Ian what's-his-name was cooling off a bit. So she told him she was pregnant. Just to make sure of him.'

'You mean she isn't really?'

'Course she isn't. She's the last person on earth to tie herself down with a child, now, isn't she? You know our dear Lori.'

'How do you know all this?'

'Well, she told me. We went to a club

one night and she got a bit drunk. We were quite close for a time. She used to pour out every blinking detail of this wedding until I was sick to the back teeth with it all. Every detail of her dress and the flowers and who was coming to the wedding of the year. I didn't even get an invite. She used to be a friend until I had to cover for her one too many times. Cheeky blighter. This Tuesday night for example, I'm just going off shift in A&E and she phones me. Pleeeeese darling, just for me. So much to do before the wedding. So much stress. And now my cousin's flown in from the States.'

'And you couldn't say no, I suppose?'

'Well, this time, I did. Then I heard she'd phoned in sick and I got called back in anyway. I was so angry. Anyway, let's get back to reception. You won't tell anyone all this stuff, will you? Sorry, I shouldn't have gone on but I was just feeling fed up. Only I promised I wouldn't let on to anyone. About her pretend pregnancy, I mean. Poor bloke.

I bet he hasn't a clue what he's in for with that one.'

Matti lay on the trolley, her jaw dropping and her temper rising. How was she going tell Ian this latest bit of news? She frowned, trying to think how she should deal with it. He was still feeling very angry and this was going to infuriate him even more.

'Miss Harper?' The doctor came in, accompanied by the nurse she'd overheard. 'How are you feeling today?'

'A bit battered. But I'm all right. I wasn't sure why I needed to come in today.'

'We took another look at your wrist x-ray. There's something we don't like the look of and I wanted to see you again.'

'But you said it was all right last night.'

'I thought you needed the rest overnight before we began manipulation again today. Mr Faulkner seemed to think you should go home and said he'd look after you.'

168

'Yes, he did. He's here with me. Well, he's just gone up to see a patient we operated on yesterday.'

'It's not you who is Lori's flatmate?' the nurse asked suddenly. She had gone quite pale.

'I am,' Matti replied with a wry grin. 'And yes, I overheard what was being said.'

'Oh how awful. I'm so sorry.' The nurse looked devastated.

'Not to worry. In this case, I'm very grateful to you but I suggest that in future, you need to be more careful. You never know who's listening.'

'Am I missing something?' the doctor asked.

'Just a bit of hospital gossip. Not that often you get a member of staff on a trolley in the next cubicle. But I might just need to get you to repeat this particular bit of gossip to someone else.'

'Can we get back to your wrist now, please?' the doctor said irritably. 'I'm going to put in a shot of local anaesthetic and re-tape it.' He studied the x-ray and then began his work. Matti lay back and tried to relax.

Once she had been finally checked over and asked a long string of questions, the doctor was satisfied.

'It may be a week or two before you can get full movement back. Then we'll try some physiotherapy for a while. I'm afraid you won't be able to work in theatre for several weeks. But light duties will be fine. Take some pain killers for when the anaesthetic wears off. Come back if you've any problems.'

'Thanks very much.'

The nurse went back to the reception area with her. Ian was sitting waiting alone.

'Sam had to go,' he said, getting up as she approached. 'Everything all right?'

'Certainly is. Ian, I'd like you to meet Nurse . . . sorry, I don't know your name. Oh, Julie. It's on your badge.'

'Hallo, Julie,' Ian said, holding out his hand. He looked questioningly at Matti.

'Julie is, or was, a friend of Lori's. Julie, this is Ian Faulkner. I'd like you to tell him exactly what you told your friend back there.'

The nurse's face contorted and she put her hand up to her mouth.

'Oh but I couldn't. I mean . . . Mr Faulkner is marrying Lori . . . tomorrow isn't it?'

Ian looked grim. 'Come on. What's going on?'

'Lori confided something to Julie. Something you need to know. Come on now, please tell him. Unless what you were saying wasn't true.'

'Oh it's true all right. Lori told me she was pretending to be pregnant just so you'd be sure to marry her. She was afraid you were thinking of changing your mind.' Julie looked away, her face red with embarrassment. Ian looked as if he were about to burst a blood vessel.

'If this is true, then there definitely will be no wedding tomorrow. I have to speak to Lori. Are you through here, Matti?'

'Yes, thanks. Shall I order a taxi to get me home?'

'Of course not. I can use your phone if Lori isn't back.'

They drove the short distance from the hospital to the flat in silence. The clenching of Ian's knuckles on the steering wheel was the only sign of his agitation and anger.

'I'm going to call Sam and ask him to come round,' she informed her companion when they returned to the flat. 'I need his support even if you don't.'

'Do you believe that girl?' he asked. 'Was she telling the truth or just stirring up trouble?'

'I believe her. She was very angry at being taken for granted when Lori got her to do extra shifts on her behalf. She wasn't even at the hen party, as she was covering. Meant she didn't know me and my connection to Lori.'

Ian dialled Lori's number. Matti was leaving the room but he called her back.

'I want you to hear what's being said.

Lori? It's me. Are you coming back to the flat?' He listened for a moment. 'I need to talk to you. I'll do it over the phone if necessary. Okay. See you in a little while. No, we'll speak face to face.' He hung up. 'She's actually on her way. I gather her parents are with her.'

'That should make for an interesting meeting. How are you going to tackle it?'

'Search me. Oh Matti, what have I done?'

'Allowed yourself to be flattered by a pretty girl and let yourself get carried away by events. Admittedly, quite out of character for you.'

'If what we've been told is true, then maybe it isn't too late for us?'

'Let's get this over with first. I'll put the kettle on for coffee. You'll have to make it, though. Actually, putting the kettle on is tricky.'

He made them both a cup just as Lori and her parents arrived. Mr Jones, a large, red-faced man, was clenching his fists at his side and was clearly a force to be reckoned with. His wife was a slight woman, rather pretty and with the same colouring as Lori. She was much quieter than her daughter and seemed somewhat intimidated by the angry man at her side.

'I gather everything in the garden isn't quite as lovely as it should be, considering we have a wedding tomorrow. And evidently Matti has something to do with it all?' he said.

'It's Lori herself who's at fault,' Ian said. 'She may have convinced you that she's the innocent victim in all of this, but Matti can vouch for the fact that Lori has brought several men back to the flat. Even after we were supposed to have been engaged. Also, she can tell you that your daughter has spent many nights away from here and Sam here will also confirm that she was out with another man only this week. Monday evening, wasn't it?'

Lori shook her head, evidently in denial.

'The night you were out with your

cousin from America, remember?' Matti finally spoke out.

'You haven't got a cousin from America, darling,' Mrs Jones said without thinking.

'Shut up, Mum. You're not helping.' Lori spoke for the first time. Ian glared at her and continued.

'Matti is not involved in any of this. However, I admit that she may well be involved in my own future. I think Lori has some explaining to do. You've been lying to me, Lori, haven't you?'

'About what? Ian, how could you treat me like this?'

'No, how could *you*? Telling me you were pregnant.'

'Lori, oh Lori, you're not, are you?' her mother burst out.

The girl looked from one to the other. 'I didn't want you to know,' she muttered.

'But you're not pregnant, are you, Lori?' Ian persisted.

'I don't know what you mean.'

'I've been speaking to Julie. Your

friend Julie. You made a confession to her.'

'The sneak. She promised not to tell anyone. No, I'm not pregnant. That should please you, Mum.'

'I came here ready to shout at you for leading my little girl on. But you're right. I think she has some explaining to do.' Mr Jones was looking grim.

Arguments raged back and forth for the next hour. Sam joined them during the final phases of the arguments and listened incredulously to what he was hearing. Eventually, the decisions were finally made. The wedding was off. A tearful Lori spoke again.

'I can't bear such a public humiliation.' Lori's voice was reaching a crescendo of emotion. 'Make him tell everyone he wants to cancel it, Daddy. And tell him he'll have to be the one to send all those gorgeous presents back. And make Matti cancel everything else. It's all her fault.'

'Of course we'll do whatever is necessary,' Sam agreed.

'Actually, there are one or two of the presents I might like to keep. We'll take them all back with us and I'll ask people what they want me to do with them,' Lori said. Ian, Matti and Sam smiled knowingly at each other. Typical behaviour from Lori.

Her parents helped her to pack her belongings together and Lori left their lives for good.

'I feel as if a huge thunderstorm has just finished,' Matti announced. 'The air is beginning to clear and life can get back to normal.'

'Pity we can't just change the bride's name to yours on the licence. Then *we* could be married tomorrow, instead.' Ian took her hand and kissed her fingertips.

'With me looking like this? I don't think so.'

'I don't care what you look like, as long as you'll marry me.'

'You sure this is not just a rebound?'

'I've just been very slow in realising the truth. So, will you marry me, Matti?'

'Of course I will. Thought you'd never ask.'

'Thank goodness something good is happening at last,' Sam told them. 'Congratulations.'

9

Over the next couple of weeks, Matti was kept busy making plans for her own wedding. She was frustrated by being unable to use her right wrist. She scribbled almost unreadable notes with her left hand but Ian and Sam were most attentive and helped whenever they could. Ian had cancelled his wedding leave and was working with another theatre sister. Matti felt jealous but he reassured her that she would never be replaced long-term.

She had been visited by the police to make a statement about the accident and the teenage driver had been charged on several counts. There had even been an article in the local newspaper. She had tried to refuse a photographer taking pictures of her but had been persuaded that it would be a useful warning to other lawbreakers.

To her great surprise, one day a parcel had been delivered to the hospital, along with a bouquet of flowers. Ian brought it round after work. The parcel contained a new red jacket and the card read:

'*We were very sorry to hear of your accident. Rory wanted you to have a new jacket to replace the one that floated out to sea when you rescued him. Hope it fits! Ever grateful to you. Love, Rory and family.*'

'How lovely of them,' Matti said almost tearfully. 'People are so kind.'

'You deserve it. People take too much for granted these days. Now, what lists have you made today? I want us to be married as soon as possible and I'm relying on you to organise it all.'

'Not many lists but I've come to several big decisions today. I've decided I'd like us to have a very small, quiet wedding. I can't cope with all the fuss and waste of some lavish affair. Seeing how stressed Lori was getting, I just want to marry you in the simplest way possible.' Ian looked somewhat non-plussed. 'Unless you'd be disappointed by that?'

'Darling Matti, I can't tell you how relieved that makes me feel. I was dreading having to go through all that decision-making all over again. Flowers and stuff leave me cold.'

'Oh, we shall have flowers. And I'm going to have a posh frock. Shall we just invite family to the ceremony? And Sam of course, and one or two close friends. But does it matter if I don't have a bridesmaid?'

'Sounds great. And we'll have a nice meal somewhere after the ceremony. One of the hotels suit you?'

'Sounds good to me.'

'I've taken the liberty of getting a licence so I suggest two weeks on Saturday if that's all right.'

'I shall still have a scar and I won't have lost this wretched sling by then. The wedding photographs will all be spoilt.'

Ian stared at her, his jaw dropping in shock. 'But I thought you didn't care about all of that?'

Matti grinned and he relaxed. 'Just winding you up. But Sam will be flashing his new digital camera and taking pictures of our every move. I can always tuck some flowers into the sling and wear a big hat to hide the scar. But we need to get moving quickly or we'll be on our own without even the family. And I really do need to buy something new to wear. Do you think Sam would take me into town? I still can't drive.'

'Don't be silly. I'll take you, of course.'

'But you can't. It would be really bad luck if you saw the outfit before the day.'

'Oh Matti, I do love you. I'm just so sorry it took so long to realise it.'

'And I love you, Ian. Forever.'

THE END

WHERE THE HEART IS
OUT OF THE BLUE
TOMORROW'S DREAMS
DARE TO LOVE
WHERE LOVE BELONGS
TO LOVE AGAIN
DESTINY CALLING

Other titles in the
Linford Romance Library:

ANNA'S RETURN

Sally Quilford

Anna Silverton and Janek Dabrowski escape war-torn Europe together, forging a friendship that carries them through difficult times. Even when they are apart, Anna dreams of Janek coming for her so they can be a family. Then, when she is accused of harming her half-brother, Teddy, she runs away, finding Janek again. Their childhood friendship soon turns to a tentative love, but the vicious lies told about Anna force them to part once again. Can the couple ever have a future together?